Love
and Other
Natural Disasters

Love
and Other
Natural Disasters

Allen Hannay

An Atlantic Monthly Press Book
Little Brown and Company
BOSTON   TORONTO

FIRST EDITION

Library of Congress Cataloging in Publication Data

Hannay, Allen.
 Love and other natural disasters.

 "An Atlantic Monthly Press book."
 Summary: Having fallen in love with the divorced
mother of his sometimes-date, nineteen-year-old
Bubber finds his life is further complicated by his
approaching parenthood.
 [1. Unmarried fathers — Fiction] I. Title.
PZ7.H19815Lo   [Fic]   81–23674
 ISBN 0–316–34362–5   AACR2

ATLANTIC–LITTLE, BROWN BOOKS
ARE PUBLISHED BY
LITTLE, BROWN AND COMPANY
IN ASSOCIATION WITH
THE ATLANTIC MONTHLY PRESS

BP
Book designed by S. M. Sherman

Published simultaneously in Canada
by Little, Brown & Company (Canada) Limited

PRINTED IN THE UNITED STATES OF AMERICA

For Sally

Book I

Chapter

1

Some discoveries set you free, but most just complicate your life. I learned this on a warm spring night when I discovered the important ligaments on Shirley Butts's chest, and solved the mystery of how a bosom holds on to a girl's body.

We were parking under the big pecan in Shirley's front yard, where we could see into the parlor window. Shirley said she wanted to park within shouting distance of her mother, in case I got wild. Also, to cool my pants, she poured a cup of Dr Pepper in my lap. I can't say she trusted me much, though it was she who had the bad reputation.

But that night was even worse than usual. Earlier in the evening Mrs. Butts had sprayed the pecan tree for tent caterpillars. As we coasted into position, engine and headlights off, the air still stung with poison.

"That bitch did this on purpose," Shirley said, rolling up the window. "If I haven't told you before, Momma's against me having sex. She definitely needs psychiatric help."

She glanced to see whether I nodded, which I did, quickly. Shirley didn't tolerate any debate about the precarious mental state of her mother.

Satisfied, she picked up her boar bristle hairbrush and began stroking her wavy blond hair. It seemed very long because she was very short — over a foot shorter than me and a hundred pounds lighter. Being petted by me she must have felt she was being trampled by a brewery horse. She looked forward to it with equal longing.

"Keep your paws off until I say okay."

"I wasn't touching, just looking. You're the prettiest girl I've ever been out with."

"Probably," she said.

We sat silently considering this. Shirley wasn't the prettiest girl in school, but she ranked herself as the best-looking junior. And though a ranking that high might deserve the lengthy, silent consideration Shirley gave it, I found myself distracted by her mother's house. It was old and decaying, and it had never been very grand — just a clapboard box at the far edge of town, where cotton farmers had once slept between chores. The best that could be said for it was that it had been a useful shelter, but even those days were nearly past. Several years ago Mr. Butts, an auctioneer, had run off to the Fort Worth stockyards with a floozy, and from the peeling white porch paint to the pile of Glad bags stacked on it, the house showed the lack of a man.

Gradually the silence was broken and my interest changed again. "Hey, what's that sound?"

"Is it her?" Shirley scooted down in the seat and pulled open her blouse. "Is she coming?"

"No, honey, it's not your mother. What are you doing?"

"Ugh," Shirley responded, sitting up.

"You sound disappointed. You wanted to get caught naked?"

"Harumpf," she said, brushing her hair again. Her blouse was still open. I could see the curve of her brassiere, a little French one.

"Shucks, I'm disappointed, too," I said, laying a careful arm around her. "I'd sure like to spend time in jail for statutory rape. But, well, we've got to get used to life's little disappointments if we want to grow up strong."

She pushed my arm away. "Shut up, Mister A Student. You may be smart, but you've got stupid big ears and a cowlick. What *is* that noise?"

A gentle patter had commenced on the car roof—a drizzle, we discovered, of falling caterpillars. The method of killing them called for torching their tents with flaming newspaper, then saturating the tree with poison. Above us the survivors of the fire were gradually losing control of their nervous systems, and dropping from the limbs to their deaths. The fall was just the right height to bust their guts on my old De Soto.

"I've got to move." I reached for the ignition. My De Soto was the last of its breed, parts were impossible to find, and when the first thing broke, the old machine would die. "Christ, the hood looks like velvet."

"Don't move, honey." Shirley touched my hand with suspicious tenderness. "If you stay here I'll let you see all of me you want. Above the waist," she added.

5

"When?" I asked immediately. Mostly Shirley promised rather than delivered.

"As soon as I finish my hair."

I sighed and rested back in the seat, watching her. After seven dates I thought I might love her; at least I loved some things about her. She wore a pleated skirt and sandals. Her hair smelled of apricot shampoo.

But waiting was painful. One moment the caterpillars would *tick . . . tick,* resembling Chinese water torture, followed by a splash of them, indicating a mass leap. The poison in the air and the mass deaths reminded me of world wars. Sitting beside Shirley also reminded me of wars; she was in one with her mother.

"Kiss me!" She threw herself between me and the steering wheel. "She's looking out the window."

In her hurry she banged our noses, and our front teeth clicked. I flinched away but she held me firmly in place by the ears. "Don't," she mumbled into my mouth, "move. If you were hurt we'd taste blood."

She persisted in kissing me like this for a very long time. Every time I moved my tongue to taste for blood she told me, "No frenching." Her mother, she was convinced, knew we were out there, knew what we were doing, and was tormented by the knowledge. I could see into the parlor and I was not convinced. Mrs. Butts had only raised the window for air, then flopped down in her La-Z-Boy to watch the *Tonight Show.* She was red-haired and green-eyed, very Irish and a little drunk. She kept dropping cigarettes and jumping up to shake them out of her robe. Finally, smoking and drinking at the same time became too dangerous, so she quit smoking.

6

Back in the car I was getting used to Shirley's face leaned up against mine, even getting to appreciate the way her apricot hair filtered the poison from the air. The *Tonight Show* guest host, Rodney Dangerfield, was delivering his monologue; a thick breeze was blowing in from the prairie; and between the splashes on the roof I could catch a few of Rodney's best lines. It was not a completely unpleasant night.

"Is she still there?"

"Yeah," I said, nestling further in her hair, "and is her face red."

Wiggling with joy Shirley couldn't resist taking a peek. When she saw I was lying she jerked down on my ears.

"Ooooh! Ahhh!"

"Some ball player you are." Shirley rearranged herself on the far side of the seat. "I hope they take your scholarship away."

"They wouldn't dare, not with my physique." I recovered enough to flex my biceps. "More muscle than a horse, but less than a pig, I like to say."

Instead of laughing, Shirley huffed. "You've got the reputation at school you deserve — weird."

My biceps sank and I slumped back in the seat. "Why? I'm just like everyone else."

"Like *who*? You live with an old man in a serpentarium. And look in the back seat — what do you see?"

I didn't need to look. "Armadillos," I said.

"Two *dead* armadillos. You're *weird*."

"They're road-kills, for my tiger. I'm trying to teach him to eat wild food, instead of Alpo. I'm preparing him for his freedom."

7

"*Weird!* And you always stink like that tiger, too."

I defended myself without energy. "Some people think growing up with wild animals is a learning experience. How many other guys do you know with a tiger?"

"Please! No more talk about that animal. Don't you have any human friends? Aren't you friends with Ransom McKnight?" She watched me.

"Handsome Ransom? Sure, he and I are buddies."

Shirley took another look at me, then stared at the dashboard. It was the sort of stare that meant the starer was making a decision that would affect your life, for the worse.

"What's the matter, hon, don't you like my smell anymore?" I laid my arm around her and sniffed her tiny ear.

"Not particularly. And stop leaning on me."

"But after the first couple of times with me you said you'd never been so happy."

She stopped brushing abruptly and turned on me. "I've told the same thing to five different guys. Jesus, didn't you even ask around about me?"

"No, I didn't think to."

"Well, think next time. You'll save yourself a lot of heartache."

I cleared my throat, stretched my neck, and thought. But there didn't seem to be a glimmer of hope for Shirley and me. I was just too nice for her.

"I guess this'll be our last date then." I tried to say this lightly, devil-may-care, but I must have said it wrong.

"God, you *are* a baby. 'I guess this'll be our last date.'"

Having my tender feelings mocked made me angry. *I'd*

8

show her who was too nice. I opened her blouse with a hand trembling only slightly. "You promised me something."

"All right, all right. Aren't you the aggressive one?" She pulled out her shirttail and unsnapped her brassiere. I bent under the front seat and found my flashlight.

"No sir, put that thing away." She lay against the far door, wide-eyed, as if she expected to bludgeoned.

"It's dark. I need it to see what I'm looking at."

"No way." She paused. I bent down to stow the Big Beam back under the seat, and she regained her control.

"Okay, I'll let you use it on one condition."

"What?"

"Get me a date for Round-up . . . with Ransom."

Round-up was the annual spring dance in Waller County. Everyone in Merry, Texas, got drunk and pretended they were out on the open range again, instead of the outskirts of Houston. This was Wednesday, and the dance was just two days away.

But I knew Randy didn't have a date; he'd recently disgraced his girlfriend Babs, the prettiest girl in school. Before she'd been sent away to live with her Baptist aunt, she'd given him all his pictures back, and it had taken both of us to carry them. Apparently Randy had given her a commemorative snapshot at every opportunity. He was curly-headed, moderately wealthy, vain, a sex fiend, and a friend of mine. He was also very hard on girls' reputations.

"It would be my pleasure to match you with Randy."

Shirley seemed satisfied with this, and I switched on the Big Beam.

"No sex," she warned.

"Don't worry. This is a purely clinical exam. You've broken the back of my passion."

"You're weird," she sniffed, looking off to the parlor window where her mother sat drinking. "You're the most perverted boy I've ever been out with."

I agreed quickly. I was too dumb to understand why, but the more perverse Shirley thought I was, the more compliant she became. Someone must have told her that in the clutches of a sex maniac the safest course was to relax.

She groaned with pleasure as I lifted the brassiere from her bosoms. Actually, there was nothing that made Shirley as passionate as being looked at closely. My hopes rose. With the blouse partially rebuttoned and the Big Beam shining up under it, her chest was lit up like a lampshade. I pressed my face to the top while my hands reached in from below.

Never, in all my experience with photos of naked ladies, had I noticed such detail in the female anatomy. Shirley's nipples were the color of the blush on a sweet Texas peach. And though her bosoms weren't great in size, they were perfect in shape, which is what a body-builder looks for in a bosom.

I held the light to the underside of one. The beam penetrated the flesh with a stunning pink glow. Important, slender, elastic and somehow feminine ligaments showed up as a shadowy net, like the rib cage in an X-ray. I was impressed. Bosoms were more than just another useful muscle. I'd never seen anything comparable—

excluding the turmoil of muscles in my tiger's shoulders. They were about equal to bosoms.

I was on the verge of asking Shirley to get down on all fours, to observe her bosoms swinging in their natural state, when there came a knock on the passenger window.

I raised my head from Shirley's blouse and established eye contact with her mother. We looked at each other. Mrs. Butts seemed baffled by what I was doing to her daughter.

Shirley began crying angrily. Pushing me away she flung open the door, narrowly missing her mother, who sidestepped with a hand over her drink.

"Go away, leave me alone! Haven't you done enough tonight?" Shirley shouted, now trying to pull the door shut. Mrs. Butts held it open with one hand and she wasn't a big woman.

"Button up your blouse and go inside," said a firm Mrs. Butts.

Shirley's bosoms were almost exposed, and her forceful mother was standing outside my car. I reached for the ignition.

"You bitch! You're ruining my life!" Shirley snatched up her purse and brush and jumped out. I turned the key one click; the red oil and generator lights came on. Shirley started to run to the porch, then stopped.

"And I hate your bathrobe. Those damned Kleenex in the pockets make you look like a kangaroo."

Mrs. Butts reached for a tissue. Shirley refused it, wiped her nose on her forearm, and ran up the porch steps. At the door she turned again.

"And I don't want any more lectures about men. I'll learn everything I need to, living with Daddy. He's gonna ask me to come — wait and see."

With that she went inside, slamming the screen door. Mrs. Butts and I listened and watched. Shirley's booming footsteps faded, an inner door slammed, and her bedroom light came on. We waited a little longer. The rainstorm of caterpillars had let up and a nice breeze from the prairie rustled the big pecan. I turned the ignition off and kicked the flashlight under the seat.

Mrs. Butts bent down at the door. "Is that you in there, Bubber Drumm?"

"Yes, ma'am." There was fruit juice and hard liquor on Mrs. Butts's breath and she held a full tumbler.

"Have you been having your way with my daughter?"

I had the impression that this line was supposed to be delivered fiercely, but Mrs. Butts sounded casual, which calmed me.

"No, ma'am, not exactly. I guess heavy petting was as far as we went, tonight."

Mrs. Butts cocked her head, questioning this answer. I was embarrassed I couldn't confess to a more successful passion.

"But you wanted to go farther, didn't you?" she asked somewhat graciously.

"Yes, ma'am, I did."

This answer didn't convince her either. She'd seen me doing something strange to her daugher and now she studied my face. What sort of teenage maniac did she have here?

As far as anyone in Merry knew, Mrs. Butts had given

up on men after the Mister ran off. He was a tall, skinny, thin-nosed man who wore flowered western shirts with the sleeves rolled high; he wasn't much of a man, and the town's sympathy naturally fell to Mrs. Butts. She had raised two daughters by herself and sent the oldest one off to San Diego as a court reporter. A registered nurse herself, she worked in the ortho ward of Prairie Memorial, where she helped old ladies to walk on their new Teflon hips. It was the sort of decent, depressing work that few people wanted but everyone admired. And because she'd done right by her girls, because she hadn't gone man-hunting like a lot of women in her place, the small-town gossips spoke of her with respect.

But apparently she'd been rolling slowly downhill in secret. Drunk on Wednesday night. Still, she was a good-looking woman, with wavy red hair, high eyebrows, and freckles that could have made her look young and lively. Tonight, however, she looked freckled and tired.

"I knew your mother, Bubber." As she spoke she leaned on the door and sipped from the tumbler. "She taught me through three grades in the old school and I have to say I loved her. She'd have been ashamed of you tonight."

Again she spoke without fierceness. She wasn't putting her heart into it and seemed to be drifting. "I remember when she took fertility drugs and had you. We all thought you'd be born retarded; she was real old for having children. Anyhow, I'm glad to see you aren't an imbecile. But didn't you used to be fat like one?"

I twisted in my seat and stared out across the car hood. It was covered with downy bodies. Fat downy bodies.

13

I had been fat until my mother died, when I was twelve. So fat that the entire town thought I was either a Moron, Imbecile, or Idiot — which were the old classifications for "exceptional children." Only my mother had believed in me and prevented them from putting me in Room 212, where the plump retarded kids spit up on their shirts. Understandably, I thought a lot of my mother.

After she died I had no protection except old Dad, and he'd pretty much withdrawn. So I had worked out hard and become muscular. What I *looked* like mattered. Now I had a football scholarship to the university, and was an Honor Roll student, a National Merit Scholar, and a member of SAPS (Scientific and Philosophic Society). But many people, like Mrs. Butts, remained skeptical.

"No, ma'am, I'm not a fat Imbecile anymore. I've risen to the level of a well-built Moron."

She looked at me a second time and laughed. "I'm sorry, Bubber. I'm too stupid for words."

"That's okay. Common mistake. Why don't you sit down? You look tired."

"Thanks." She sat on the edge of the seat. "I am pooped. And I don't want to go in and face her yet." We both stared at Shirley's window.

After a time she said, "I do remember you, though. I think about your family almost every day."

"You do?" I asked, surprised.

"On the way to the hospital, I do. I drive right by your daddy's serpentarium. But I've never stopped."

She mentioned this as proof of good character, like men claim they've never contacted a social disease.

"You ought to come in sometime. Dad's got a good

disposition for an old vet, and it's a very clean serpentarium."

"I'm sure."

She crossed her legs and leaned back, looking at the
ceiling fabric. "Once, about three or four years ago, I saw
you inside the tiger's cage, between the gas pumps."

"Yes?"

"And you two were wrestling. I slowed down — at first
I thought he was killing someone — then I saw it was a
husky boy rolling over and over with a tiger. I don't know
why, but that picture has stuck with me, driving to work.
I slow down every time."

Bengal and I hadn't wrestled in years. But it bothered
me that Mrs. Butts remembered me husky; I wanted her
to carry a prettier picture of me.

"We still wrestle," I said, "only I get up later now."

"I'd hoped you were — you both seemed to be enjoying
yourselves. But now when I pass he's just sleeping in that
sling chair of his."

"Yes, ma'am. Dad says a cage breaks a wild animal's
spirit. They get lazy and lose their love of life."

"I can understand that," she said simply, then grew
thoughtfully silent. She looked pretty, thoughtful.

We sat awhile longer watching Shirley's window and
listening to the pecan rustle. I kept thinking that Mrs.
Butts remembered me in my former condition.

"Well, Bubber," she said finally, "it's been nice talking
to you, but now I've got to go in and shout at my
daughter." Making no move to leave she lifted her tumbler
to the light, saw how much was left, and drank it in a
swallow.

'If you'd like," I said, "you can stop by in the morning and watch Bengal and me wrestle up close. You don't have to go inside the serpentarium."

She thought about it. "That's nice of you. I might. Yes, I think I would like to see that." Then she slapped her knee, uncrossed her legs, and stepped out of the car a little too carefully. Holding on to the roof she bent down again. Her bathrobe had come open a little, and her deep, astonishing cleavage showed. It was as if she were on all fours. Large parts of her bosoms were freckled!

"I'm sorry about these worms on your car. I thought they'd keep her from spying on me."

"Heck, the car's not important. Those worms'll blow right off."

"I'm sure," she said and weaved her way to the sagging porch steps. When she opened the screen door, Shirley's bedroom light went out. I guess Shirley wanted to pounce on her mother in the dark. I leaned out the window and called after her.

"See you in the morning. And you don't look like a kangaroo."

"Thanks," she called back in a whisper. "You don't look like a moron."

Chapter

2

As a family unit, Mom, Dad and I had been as happy as chubby cattle ticks, but after Mom passed our lives deflated rapidly. Within a week of the funeral Dad had retired from his practice as a vet, bought the old limestone service station/grocery store on the Interstate, converted it to a service station/serpentarium, and had given me a tiger cub. He seemed to think that raising a tiger would teach me all I needed to know about Life — so he wouldn't have to — and that the snakes would keep most people away. Because, while Dad liked these simple, unusually healthy, rat-eating animals, they weren't too popular with the general public anymore. In his ample free time old Dad read, studied, and brooded over his new passion, which he called The Natural Order of Things. I didn't interfere, except to tease him; when Dad studied and brooded he didn't drink so much — except on Tuesday, Wednesday, and Thursday nights.

On those nights he and his pal Sinclair Cznek felt safe enough to get drunk at the Texas Pride Domino Parlor. On the weekends, Dad explained, it wasn't safe to drink and drive, what with the less experienced drunks on the road. After the games the two old pals careened home in Sinclair's battered pickup, singing "Shoo, Shoo the blue-tailed fly, my master's gone away" at the top of their lungs while they wrestled over the steering wheel. Dad thought his friend drove like a wild, bowlegged Bohemian, and Sinclair claimed Dad drove like an old lady. They were both in their seventies and as stubborn as fenceposts.

That Wednesday night, after my date, I was outside of the serpentarium spraying Bengal with the high-pressure hose. Bengal, like most tigers, loved the water, and he leaped and frolicked in the foam. But he stopped at the same time I did, both of us recognizing the banging cylinders of Sinclair's truck far across the prairie. Its headlights leaped from one side of the ranch road to the other but stayed roughly between the bar ditches, until they hit the pea-gravel parking lot at home. There, they ran down our mailbox and slid sideways to a stop in a plume of whistling gravel. Sinclair had retired from the sheriff's department and liked to make sliding stops.

Dad threw himself out the door and leaned against the dented fender, breathing hard. He was a round-shouldered old fellow, groundhoggish by disposition. His hat had been knocked askew and his rat-nest eyebrows were tangled. He stuck out his tongue and touched it.

"Durn you, Sinclair! You made me bite myself!"

"Hell, you shouldn't of been wearing teeth. I don't, when I drive."

Lanky Sinclair stepped around to the front and checked the damage to the grill. He valued his tough Dodge truck, but he'd had fun running down a mailbox; reckless driving had been a habit of his youth. He dropped to his hands and knees.

"Hot damn and tar fire!" he hooted. "Look at that box! Reminds me of Long Roy Higgin's nose, the night I brought him in. He had a good reputation with his fists, but I had a gun." His voice drifted off, then turned wistful. "I was twenty-two back then, twenty-two years old, and I could spit fifteen feet."

"Well," Dad said, still mad, "today you can hardly spit on your own feet." He got creakily down with Sinclair. The box was pinned under the truck. Its crushed state made Dad even madder; this Bohemian misfit had nearly killed him, and struck down his mailbox too. He rocked back and smacked Sinclair on the arm.

Sinclair looked surprised; he'd been calmly reminiscing as always, and his friend had hit him. He wallowed to his knees and swung at Dad.

I didn't bother to stop the fight; neither old boy was spry enough to knock the other's hat off, and they both enjoyed the exercise. After they got winded from swinging they started grappling and gurgling, and when they were completely worn limp they dragged themselves up by the truck fender and lugged their old bones inside.

"Just remember who quit first," Sinclair said, limping behind. A formerly tall man, he wore a pencil-thin mustache and still maintained a sexually active reputation with the Waller County widows.

"Shut up," Dad replied. "I'm through fighting with you forever. When you had me down there, temporarily, you bit my arm. A man ought to take his teeth out when he fights."

Dad dumped himself into his leaking, overstuffed chair beside the wood stove, and slapped his boots up on the ottoman. Sighing deeply, he looked around at his den. The front room, full of his snakes locked safely in their snakequariums, pacified him. Let's see, he muttered to himself, which magazine would he read, now that he'd miraculously made it home? He subscribed to about forty publications, which, stacked six feet deep around his chair, resembled the strata in sedimentary rock. He slipped on his slender reading glasses and picked up the new issue of *Smithsonian*. But the entire magazine seemed devoted to the migration of the Monarch butterfly — a majestic phenomenon no doubt, but fighting had put him in a simpler mood. He tossed that magazine down and picked up the *National Enquirer* instead. There was an article in here he'd been meaning to read, about the lurid and previously unknown love affairs of Lucille Ball. Who would have thought? Lucille Ball?

Meanwhile Sinclair was at a loss, not having his pal to argue with. He wandered up and down the aisles, feeling neglected and criticizing snakes.

"They ain't got all their parts, is my main objection. Look at this fellow here. He's missing his arms, which bothers me — but hell, the worst is, he ain't even got *shoulders.*"

Dad looked up from his article. "Neither do you, anymore. It amazes me how your shirts stay on, the way your shoulders have shrunk."

"Shit." Sinclair squared himself. "At least *I* can still dance. That's more'n a fossil like you can say. You used to do it pretty good."

"I can still trot rings around you."

"Yeah, well prove it. Get up here and put a load on your legs."

Dad shook his head and several chins, then crimped his messy eyebrows down. He couldn't believe he'd kept such a crazy friend so long. Sinclair had started doing a polka by himself.

"I got a feeling, Sinclair, you're gonna mention your sister's name again — and I *don't* want to hear it."

"Claudine?" Sinclair stopped dancing. "Why'd I mention her? She's just the best cook in the county and one of the few good dancing partners left alive. Hell, you must be thinking about her, you brung her name up."

"I've heard it every five minutes all night," Dad grumbled. "But I've still got enough sense to avoid Bohemian women, especially her. Waitressing in a beer joint, at her age!"

"Why you uptight old turkey," Sinclair said, getting mad. In Texas, Bohemian families are close. "To think I give up a date with a liberated brown-eyed fifty-five-year-old, to hear my flesh and blood insulted."

"The door's wide open," Dad offered. "Nothing's stopping you but arthritis. And I don't give a durn if I ever play dominoes with you again, the way you played tonight."

"Well, you may not — at least not tomorrow night. I'm cutting hay with Lucy Taylor, while I still can."

Dad rattled his *Enquirer*. "A Classic Second Adolescence. I read about it two issues ago."

"Yeah, well, you keep *reading* about it."

Sinclair hitched up his trousers, which the polka had

pushed down a bit, and stomped off toward the front door. But he stopped short. He didn't really want to go home yet; he had lived in the noisy Lost Pines Trailer Court since he lost his wife Eustace in the house fire, and it seemed that at night his footsteps in the trailer made a disturbing, hollow sound. He wiped his mouth, probably thinking it would be easier to sleep if he was drunker.

Loops, our twenty-foot reticulate python, came oozing across the linoleum in front of him. Loops was the only snake allowed to roam free, and he was a persistent, unsuccessful rat hunter. Sinclair touched him contemplatively with his boot.

"Now this snake I could like. If he had ears, he'd almost have a face."

Dad grunted from behind his magazine. It was a friendly grunt and Sinclair felt encouraged enough to ask for a cold beer.

"Help yourself," Dad said. "They're probably not cold, though. My icebox is more broke down than you."

While Sinclair clomped down the connecting hall to the kitchen, Dad stepped outside. I was drying purring Bengal through the bars with a towel; in many ways, he was not the picture of a ferocious jungle beast. But then, I had babied him since he was the size of a shoebox. Dad, however, didn't approve.

"Be careful, boy. You're liable to be the one-armed owner of a tiger."

"Aw," I said, "he's not gonna turn on me." To prove it I stuck my nose down his ear. Wet, Bengal's aural membranes smelled rich, like carrot cake.

Dad watched me sourly. "From your expression," he

said, "I'd say you were smelling flowers. Your date with that other carnivore must have gone pretty well."

Dad was always extremely interested in my dates; he believed I fornicated on every one. I enjoyed teasing the old guy.

"Yeah," I said in a voice that indicated sweet memories, "the last part especially. And I don't think Shirley got too pregnant."

Snorting, Dad disappeared around the corner of the building. Few things made him madder than loose morals. According to him, morals were the important difference between animals and Homo sapiens.

"You're awful uptight," I called after him. I could hear him pissing in his usual spot. "But women don't have to wear white gloves in public anymore. They've been liberated — they've got the 'Pill.' "

"Durn you!" Dad hollered. "You made me sprinkle my boots. A man don't talk about women like that. There's no two ways about it."

Long-legged Sinclair stepped outside then and gave me a wink over his can of Pearl beer. He could see that I'd gotten under Dad's skin and wanted to join me there.

"Bubber's right, Charlie. Women have finally changed, thank the Lord. Even your favorite one — Dinah Shore — she's shacked up with a younger man."

"Durn you, Sinclair!"

Sinclair grinned. "I bet he sprinkled his trousers, too."

Dad came hustling back, wet to the knees. He was mad at both of us, but also at Dinah Shore. He'd been a faithful watcher of her show — and still was — but he felt she'd betrayed her special grace when she opened her arms to that slick country boy, Burt Reynolds. He'd thought of all sorts of explanations, though.

"I got that whole thing figured out, for the information of you two sex maniacs. Dinah and Burt were driven together by their hormones."

Sinclair nearly choked, laughing on a mouthful of Pearl, and I couldn't help snickering myself. Dad always went back to hormonal drives to explain behavior; that's how the Monarchs knew their way south, wasn't it?

"Go ahead, you two; laugh at an old vet. But I'm right. Younger fellas, older ladies — that's how it works in Nature; one of the sexes always wants to procreate."

"Pro-create?" Sinclair had to hold on to the Coke machine, to keep from laughing himself to the ground. "Is that what Dinah wanted to do?"

Dad started hopping, he was so mad, and I stood up to calm him. When the old fellow lost his head like this, he often kicked chairs and hurt his feet. I put my arms around him and gave him a strong hug. But he was having none of that tonight.

"Turn loose of me! You're going homosexual — you muscle freak — gonna shame the family name."

"Aw, don't worry about that." I kept a grip on him. "I only like ladies: They make less noise when they spit."

Dad was still hopping, but he laughed a little and settled down in my arms. Actually, he was at an age where he liked to be hugged. He swatted my arm a couple of times, affectionately.

"All right, all right, my blood pressure's back near normal."

After he'd gone back inside I walked Sinclair to his

pickup. He wasn't as good a beer drinker as he'd once been and needed some help.

"Are you okay to drive?"

"Hell, yes," he said, falling into the seat and drawing his long legs in behind. "Besides, I got this automobile trained."

But in the doorlight his face looked weary, especially around the eyes. Setting his teeth on the dashboard, he rummaged through the ashtray.

"I put them damned keys in here somewhere, I know that."

"They're in the ignition, Sinclair."

"Oh. Yeah." He started the rumbling truck, then set his hat back on his head, to let his hair breathe. "You tell Charlie he's taking my sister to the dance, even if I have to bait him there with whiskey."

"You may have to."

"I know it," Sinclair muttered. "He's completely given up on the ladies since Abby passed on, and if he don't get with them quick—" Sinclair made a cutting motion across his throat. "Use it, or lose it — ain't that what the song says?"

"I don't think it's that serious. He just needs time."

"Time?" Sinclair snorted. "Time's just what old men and young boys don't have. But hell, why am I talking to you? The both of you is cut from the same mold; you got two left feet in matters of women."

"Now," I said, "I'm a little better than Dad."

"Yeah?" Sinclair pulled his hat down a notch and looked me over. "Sure you are. What'd Shirley do, pour another Dr Pepper in your lap?"

I took a few steps back. "I'll talk to Dad tomorrow, about the dance."

"You do that. And talk up my sister some. She's already dyed her hair the color of Dinah's."

"She has?" I asked, surprised. "I saw her in the Piggly Wiggly last week; she was a chestnut brunette."

"Hell, widows change ever' other week—don't you even know *that?*" Sinclair put the truck in gear and lowered his hat to the eyebrows. "Well, I'm off to fight crime," he said, and gunned out of the pea-gravel without his headlights. I shouted to him but he didn't hear, then I ran out to the ranch road and listened. But there were no loud crashes or fiery explosions, only a lonely cow lowing out on the prairie pasture, and the distant sound of a diesel John Deere.

The field across from our house was in rice, and this time of year, before the heavy rains, Mr. Jim Darrow loosened the sod with his Scotch bottom plow. Next he'd disc, cultivate, fertilize, and seed—every spring the same comfortable cycle of chores. I stuffed my hands in my pockets and walked back to talk to Bengal, but after I'd sat down on the Goodyear display beside him, we both grew silent and watched. Far out across the field, where the big prairie stars and planets lay down to the flat horizon, we could see the lights of the big tractor, freshening the soil for the seed. It seemed to us a very good time of year.

Rash promises made during idle conversation should not be kept, I discovered in the morning. It was an extremely foggy dawn, with a layer rising thickly from the ground to the windowsill of my little attic bedroom. It was as if I were on a cloud. Far off toward town only the peaks of roofs, the domes of the town pecans, and the rice dryer poked through. Out in the rice field Mr. Jim Darrow was now discing, and a line of black diesel smoke rose out of the fog.

Downstairs I ate a hurried breakfast of bananas and buttermilk. Off the kitchen Dad snored in his bedroom, and under the sink Loops poked around, hunting our spotted house-rats, Pierce and Magnolia. But as usual they were safely on the table sorting through the tin tray of my last night's TV dinner. Dad and I ate on independent schedules because Dad had turned lazy when he retired. About ten he'd wake up, eat some bran cereal and mineral oil, then spend the rest of the morning waiting for the eruption. I was glad to be away at school. By afternoon he felt as fit as a fifty-year-old and when I got home after workout, he was still pounding his chest. Toward supper time, though, his age got to him; but once he stuffed down a supper of ranch beans and aspirin he felt ready for a domino game. Both he and Sinclair had worked hard all their lives, through many wars and the Great Depression, but they never felt younger than they did whipping the pants off opponents at Texas 42. Now, of course, Sinclair was dating more, and the evenings had wilted a bit.

Outside, the headlights of cars on the Interstate moved slowly in the uncertain weather. Bengal lay in his sling chair, surprised to see me unlocking his cage door and stepping quickly inside. This was a mistake. I stepped right into Bengal's neat pile of feces.

"Yuck," I said, scraping off my tennis shoe.

Bengal growled. He was fond of his neat feces pile.

27

"Come on, you degenerate. Let's get sweated up before the lady arrives."

I took off my T-shirt and tossed it out of the cage. Bengal blinked his yellow eyes, like he did when he tried to remember something. It must have been a year since we'd wrestled regularly, ever since I'd started wrestling with girls. But back then we'd done it often, and I must say that Bengal had taught me most of the moves I now used to block energetic linebackers. In a way, I owed my football scholarship to my tiger.

"That's right." I clapped my hands and circled behind his sling chair. "Three rounds, starting *now!*"

With a swift move I dumped him out of the chair, and he rolled to his feet with all the grace of a ripple sent through a garden hose. Then he came at me with his great head low, the tip of his tail flicking, and without a pause in his stride he crouched and leaped. Apparently he remembered how to wrestle dirty.

His forepaws hit my shoulders and carried me down as though my ankles were hinged. My breath was knocked out. His feet pinned my shoulders and legs. He stooped over my face, bumping my forehead with the tender pink tip of his nose. Then raising up he let out a volcanic roar. The bones in my skull seemed to vibrate.

"Off! Off!" I commanded, as soon as my breath came back. I have a deep voice when I yell, and surprised, Bengal obeyed. He climbed off me and before I cooled down I jumped up to grab him by the waist. A tiger's hips are his weakest point, and I floored him quickly, then lifted him by the hindlegs and drove him around the cage like a wheelbarrow. After a half-dozen circuits his power-ful front-end grew weak, supporting all his weight. I let him slump to the ground, growling, and jumped on him belly to belly, pretending to bite his neck.

For the next several minutes we rolled together, spar-ring with our jaws and batting each other joyfully in the head. This was the scene Mrs. Butts had remembered. Bengal stunk with the famous stink of tigers, and gradual-ly I did, too. My arms swelled and grew hard with blood; I only wished Mrs. Butts could see me alive like this.

After a time, though, Bengal's snarls grew serious; living five years in a cage had made him cranky. When he batted my head a little too hard I rolled onto my feet and stepped quickly away, facing Dad. He held the high-pressure hose, his free hand on the cage door. Bengal lay somewhere behind me.

"He's crouched." Dad's voice was not loud, but not calm either. "Keep looking at me and move slow, to the door."

I sensed Bengal coiled behind me; I seemed to see him through a third eye. Maybe I was seeing him in Dad's eyes; I'd never looked into them so intently.

Then Bengal scooted up a few paces — I distinctly heard him. My scalp tried to crawl to a small spot on the top of my head; my straining ears seemed to face back-wards. Bengal was hunting me.

"*Don't* look behind you," Dad repeated. "If he thinks you see him, he'll attack. Just *move*."

I hadn't moved a step! I took two painfully slow ones, and rested. My heart knocked; I couldn't breathe. Taking another step, I turned my head slightly, trying to catch Bengal in my peripheral vision. That was when he pounced.

He hit me with most of his four hundred pounds on my shoulders. I pitched forward and bounced on the concrete. Pinning me, Bengal extended his front claws and ran them down my jeans in one long, rather delicate stroke; then he peeled them off my leg like a banana skin. One of his claws accidentally sliced my flesh, too, and he stooped to lick the blood. He seemed to like the taste, because next he began to nibble my skin. The world *taste* had never frightened me before. Bengal *tasted* me.

I saw my death and imagined the funeral service for my remains — my skull and the soles of my feet. Those were the only parts a maneater didn't eat. To bury any more of me they'd have to sweep up the piles in the corners. "These tiger feces," Reverend Sunday would say, "are all we have left of Bubber's midsection. Shall we bow our heads?"

I began to kick and squirm; I wasn't the type to be eaten lying down. Bengal, accustomed to consuming dead food, was confused and angered by this wiggling meal. Fortunately, he got mad at the wrong end of me, attacking and biting off my sneaker. Munching on it, he retreated a few paces to examine the contents.

Before he could realize his mistake and return for the foot, I sprinted for the cage door. Dad turned the water on then, and under its protective cover I fell out the door onto Dad's bedroom slippers. Bengal hadn't chased me, happy as he was to be sprayed. He leaped on my sneaker in a puddle.

Dad shut the water off, closed the door, and took a look at my leg. He was accustomed to animal-related injuries and wasn't too worried. "How you feel?"

I tried to say something but only managed to squawk. Dad tied his bathrobe sash around my calf and nodded.

"It's okay, son. What you're feeling is Man's First Fear: the fear of being food. But you'll need stitches, that's all." He stood up again and appraised Bengal, who lay in a shallow puddle purring like a chainsaw and chewing on the wet tongue of my sneaker.

"How many armadillos did you give him last night?"

"Two," I panted. Bengal was swallowing my sneaker tongue.

Dad rubbed his uppermost chin thoughtfully. "Well, if he was my tiger, I'd start feeding him *four*."

Chapter

3

PRAIRIE MEMORIAL WAS A SMALL COUNTRY hospital with a bad reputation. The reason for this was that the doctors were dangerous. The young ones, completing their residency out here, learned their craft by trial and error until they were skilled enough to earn money in the cities; and the older ones avoided the retirement blues by finding things to do in the operating rooms. Also, the hospital was not clean. Every year, at least, a staph infection swept the wards, weeding out the weak patients. As I approached this building across the flat coastal prairie I imagined a host of eager young germs and doctors yearning for me.

Today, however, the doctors were earning their keep. There had apparently been a large auto accident on the foggy Interstate, and the emergency drive was clogged with ambulances, their engines running and lights rotating. Orderlies pulled stretchers from the tailgates at a run, while nurses checked each victim at the doors, sorting the abrasions from the broken bones. Upstairs in the wards, patients left their beds to look out the windows, holding their gowns closed behind them, and hospital employees deserted their posts to lounge on the lawn, watching the commotion.

I looked for Mrs. Butts among the crowd. I was certain she'd driven past the serpentarium while Bengal was eating me, and an explanation seemed in order. Not finding her outside, I limped up to eavesdrop on two overweight nurses. They were enjoying a yogurt break.

"What did that driver say happened?" one asked. She was old, but had baby blue eyes. "I wasn't listening."

"You never listen, Claire. That's the problem of your life. You ought to be more attentive to the world around you, like me."

"I can't help it. It's an inner ear problem. Hereditary, I think."

"He said," she told Claire in a loud voice, "that an army troop truck had flipped over in a bar ditch. Crushed all those young boys."

"Oh, yes," Claire said, examining a blueberry in her yogurt. She seemed disappointed with its size.

"What do you mean, 'Oh, yes'? You didn't hear a word I said."

"I did so. You said they was multiple fractures and contusions."

"I did *not!* The driver said that. It's impossible to talk to someone like you!"

"Excuse me," I said. "Do you ladies know which floor the ortho ward is on?"

The superior nurse pointed at me. "*He* can hear me, Claire, and he's not even part of our conversation." She turned and looked me over with her bifocals. "You don't need ortho, son, you need emergency. I'll take you. And Claire, you stay right here. I don't want you getting lost again."

She was a big, barrel-chested woman, and she clamped on to my elbow like the bite of a horse, steering me to the emergency door.

Inside, the emergency bay was filled with moaning soldiers. A few sat up on their stretchers and compared dislocated wrists, but most just clutched their broken bones and moaned. To prevent them from pulling at their wounds, the orderlies tied their hands to the rails, which gave the soldiers more reason to moan. As I made my way through them to the front desk — where a frosty-looking, middle-aged nurse sat — the orderlies shoved me and the nurses glared at me with contempt. I looked like a loafer; I could still walk. I arrived at the desk ashamed of my wound.

"Pardon me, ma'am."

"Yes?" She did not look up from her neat stack of forms. Her desk top was as impeccable as her uniform, and she was trying hard not to notice the chaos on the other side.

"I have a problem with my leg. . . . Maybe I should come back later, when you're not so busy."

"Don't talk nonsense," she snapped, with her head down. "Are you bleeding? If so, please stand on the mat."

I moved to the mat. She looked up. Bleeding interested her.

"Fill out this form. Don't mark in the area reserved for office use. If you haven't brought a pen, you may use this one, but you must return it. I'm sick and tired of patients

34

running off with hospital pens." She handed me a clean ball-point and a crisp form.

I took them and looked for a place to write. But the waiting area was filled, too. An unconscious sergeant lay on the coffee table with his tongue out, and the couch was occupied by two semiconscious privates wrapped in each other's arms. Their entanglement seemed less for affection than for balance, and I decided it was unsafe to move them. When I tried to write against the wall, the ball-point lost its ink. Each time I stopped to shake it, the desk nurse glared at me. Was I breaking hospital pens?

I returned the form and she glanced at it. Then she read it again, carefully.

"What is this — the nature of your injuries?"

"A few tiger scratches."

She checked each line again, putting the details together. Finally she read my name and address.

"Bubber Drumm!" She looked up and smiled. "I was in your mother's class in the old school."

She examined me curiously. I anticipated her.

"No ma'am, I'm not a moron. But I did used to be fat like one."

She bent over the form, embarrassed. "Please take a seat. A doctor will see you in a moment."

A moment meant two hours, I found. I stood for a while, trying not to bleed where people stepped, and when a nurse removed one of the privates I took his place on the couch. The remaining private fell against my shoulder, whimpering again and again, "Louise, I strayed, but I paid." Other soldiers moaned on all sides, while nurses shouted back and forth. "Hemostatic clamp, STAT!" — "Tibia? Fibula?" — "I'm checking, give me a minute, will you?" — "Ouch! Ouch!"

I became disoriented and imagined that this was Hell. And the nurses were devilettes who prepared the broken bodies for the fires. I must have been feverish, because they had to call my name a dozen times before I realized that "a moment" was over.

A soft-spoken, sweet-smelling young nurse steered me to a bed behind a curtain. The doctor waited with his back turned, writing on a small stainless-steel table. His white coat was yellow and its sidepockets bulged with about twenty assorted candy bars.

"Ambulatory?" he asked without turning.

"Yes, Dr. Frank, but he's not an accident."

"Oh?" he said, still writing.

"This one is tiger bites."

"Oh?" he asked with more interest.

When he turned around I saw he was a very young man with a mustache to make him look older. There was something more remarkable about him, though. He held his watery blue eyes wide open. Completely open. It was the contagious sort of expression that made everyone around him try it out. I opened my eyes wide, and so did the nurse, but we closed them quickly because it was also the sort of expression that caused violent headaches. I looked at Dr. Frank again. His fingernails weren't clean, and the ends of his stethoscope were waxy. I decided he was high on candy, crippled by migraines, and covered with germs. I tried to get up.

He pushed me down and examined the wounds on my

calf with a sharp pair of tweezers. "This long laceration —
must have been a large tiger?" He nudged me in the ribs
and laughed.

I had never seen a man laugh with his eyes wide open,
and it worried me. The nurse lay a hand on my shoulder,
both to comfort me and to hold me in place.

"At any rate," the doctor said, becoming immediately
serious, "Nurse Walker, a tetanus booster and eight cc's
Cyclaine. And I'll need a 2-o silk on a cutting needle." He
turned his open eyes back to me. "Please lay on your
stomach and relax. We'll have you sewn together in a
jiffy."

I don't know how long a jiffy lasted, but it was in the
neighborhood of an hour. I encouraged Dr. Frank to take
his time, though. He began by having trouble pinching
hold of the needle, and while he worked he muttered,
"Oh, shit," from time to time. Sweat from his brow
sprinkled my leg; I was certain it contained lethal germs.

Afterwards, in the corridor, I couldn't resist peeling
back the bandage for a look. The stitches weren't pretty,
and they were only slightly tighter than the laces on a
football. But all things considered I felt lucky that Dr.
Frank hadn't sewn Nurse Walker's hand to my leg.

Limping down the corridor I began looking for Mrs.
Butts again. I found her pushing a gurney out of a door
marked X-RAY. An unconscious, fragile old lady lay on the
gurney with a fresh-smelling cast on her hips. A bag of
plasma hung from a pole and dripped down a hose into
her arm.

Mrs. Butts wore her white uniform and a cap to match,
with her wavy red hair pinned back. Her stockings made

37

a crisp, electric sound as she walked; her bosoms looked large; she was much prettier than I remembered.

Before I could speak, a short X-ray technician with blow-dried hair stuck his head out the door. "This is the last time I make allowances for you. A patient must be zapped *before* surgery."

"What difference does it make? Dr. Sagus can't read the plates anyway."

"All right, all right, that's enough. I play bridge with the doctor; I won't hear a word against him. I'm calling Mrs. White to report your infraction."

"You do that, you bug."

He slammed the door and Mrs. Butts straightened her cap. She patted the old lady's arm, and pushed on toward me. I said hello.

"Hello," she said, adding tentatively, "Bubber?"

"Yes, ma'am, Bubber Drumm." I wanted to put her at ease. "You only saw me in the dark, and you were pretty tired."

She smiled. "Today I'm tired; last night I was hog-drunk. But thank you, Bubber."

There followed an awkward silence. She didn't act as though she'd seen Bengal tasting me, and I didn't want her to know he had. She felt guilty too easily as it was, and she would just feel responsible for the accident.

"Wasn't I supposed to stop at the serpentarium this morning? I'm sorry."

"That's okay. It's just well you didn't." She pushed the gurney down the hall, with me following trying not to limp. "You were probably late or something."

"That's true, I was late, but the truth is I completely

forgot." She glanced at me guiltily. "And if you weren't supposed to be in school, I'd make it up to you with a cup of coffee."

"Oh, I'm not missing much; I'd like some coffee." I surprised her by accepting, but I gave her a way out. "But I can see you're busy right now." I nodded back toward the X-ray door.

"Oh, that pest. George thinks he's the only one here who knows his job. But every time I come down his work is stacked up and he's busy trimming his nostril hairs in the mirror."

"Well," I consoled her, "those X-rays will probably make him sterile, so at least he won't be able to reproduce."

"That's a thought." She laughed, and looked at me as though she were remembering someone else. "Your mother had a sense of humor, too," she said. "I don't know why Shirley went out with you, though. She doesn't know how to laugh."

I nodded, realizing that I'd never actually heard Shirley laugh. She just said *ha, ha* at different volumes, depending on how funny she thought the joke was. Looking at Mrs. Butts, I wondered what I'd ever seen in Shirley. Mrs. Butts's freckles resembled the speckles on sparrow eggs. We were walking along pushing the unconscious lady; the plasma bag slapped against its pole.

"How rude of me," Mrs. Butts said, making a joke herself. "Bubber, I'd like you to meet Mrs. Appel. Mrs. Appel, Bubber Drumm. You remember his mother?"

"Of course she does." I bent over Mrs. Appel's face and touched her cool hand. "Enchanted."

39

Mrs. Butts was delighted. She was a woman who needed to laugh, and she seldom got the chance at Prairie Memorial. "Come on, let's find a quiet place for Mrs. Appel. She needs to rest, and *I* need some coffee."

We found an empty room, left Mrs. Appel with her dripping bag, and took the elevator down to the staff cafeteria in the basement.

The worst thing about the staff cafeteria was the staff. About half the doctors and nurses wore their whites, but the other half wore their green surgical gowns and slippers. The gowns were splashed with blood, and from the slippers it looked like they'd been wading in it. One gray-headed doctor dozed in a plastic chair in the corner, his surgical mask across his chest like a bib. Mrs. Butts went over and took a lighted cigarette from his fingers. He didn't wake up. Getting back in line with me, she said, "Dr. Sagus."

A young blood-soaked nurse with frizzy hair stopped to talk on her way out.

"How'd he do today?" Mrs. Butts asked.

"Fine, just fine. She may heal, but probably with scar tissue. I think his incision was too deep again. He gets tired so easily." She looked toward Dr. Sagus, who was sleeping like a drugged baby.

"Yes, yes," Mrs. Butts said sarcastically, "the poor man. It's *so* tiring standing up. Luckily few of his patients can do it anymore."

We got coffee and sat at a table by ourselves. Mrs. Butts was in a grumpy mood but tried to act pleasant.

"It's bad coffee, isn't it?"

"I don't know," I said, putting my cup down. "I'm not

40

really drinking any. Coffee makes me go to the bathroom."

She laughed and looked at me in an appreciative way, but I found myself distracted. At the next table a blood-stained surgeon ate a plate of liver and onions. He was very picky about cutting the pieces just so. I watched him chew, and swallow. Not very long ago I'd been food myself. I didn't feel any sudden pity or understanding for the liver, but the idea of food repulsed me. I was surrounded by people eating; most of them had been, up until lunchtime, cutting up other humans. When they looked at a patient they probably saw dotted lines, like a butcher's anatomy of a cow. I began to feel like meat.

I couldn't explain these feelings to Mrs. Butts, who asked, "What's wrong? Why are you looking at your arm like that?"

"I don't know exactly," I said. "I'm having some trouble at home." I paused. This subject would lead to Bengal, which would lead to his breakfast, so I added, "And my mother died here."

Mrs. Butts grew quiet, thinking of something to say. "That's funny," she said finally. "I can usually match people with their cause of death, but I can't remember your mother's. I must have blocked it out."

"It was cancer — I don't know what kind. They wouldn't tell me, so I guess it was one of the kinds women get."

"Well, she was a fine woman, Bubber. She helped me out quite a bit, and I wasn't the only one. It was a big funeral, wasn't it?"

I agreed. Mr. Moss, the mortician, had to borrow extra chairs from Reverend Sunday's church, and we held the services outside under the churchyard pecan. Almost all of Mom's old students came. Each one thought she'd treated him special.

I'd only visited her once in the hospital. She was jolly that day, because the February sun shone through the windows and heated her bed. Her bare feet stuck out of the sheets, as usual. She said she liked them out there, cooling her blood like a radiator. While she and I talked about school work, Dad sanded the corns on her toes with a pumice stone. He could only bear to look at her feet, because unlike her body they weren't swollen. She was hooked up to several buzzing machines with yellow hoses, and I remember thinking she looked like a Saturn rocket connected to the launch pad. Later that week, when she died, I imagined the steaming hoses breaking away, and her body lifting slowly into orbit.

Mrs. Butts changed the subject. "What troubles are you having at home?" She thought this would be more pleasant to talk about.

I was saved from having to answer by a young, oval-faced doctor with long hair. He leaned over Mrs. Butts's shoulder, his hair falling into hers, and growled.

"How's the wickedest nurse on the third floor today? Too much of the grape last night, eh?"

"Hello, Dr. Shorts." She stirred her coffee.

"Is that all I get — 'Hello, Dr. Shorts'? Time's running out for us, you know. I've only got four more months in this hellhole, before I go back to Minneapolis."

"We'll all miss you, I'm sure." She continued stirring.

"I've missed you, too," he said, "completely. How about going to the big dance with me? I drove through town this morning and those rednecks are really getting it together for Round-up. I think I even saw a legendary cowpoke or two. What do you say? I'll wear my chaps and nothing else."

"You're too much, Dr. Shorts, and what a sense of humor. Don't you agree, Bubber?" She wasn't laughing. I nodded grimly and said:

"She's already going out with me."

"I see." Dr. Shorts straightened up.

Mrs. Butts winked at me. "And please pass the word among the staff: I only go out with men under the age of twenty."

"That way we're *both* at our sexual peaks," I added, flexing my neck.

"I'll pass the word," he said stiffly, "that you're still unavailable. But really, Rose, you have to come out sooner or later. You can't let a bad marriage ruin your life." He flashed me an ugly look and left.

Mrs. Butts lifted her spoon and shook it like a thermometer. I expected her to say, "Men!" but instead she said, "Gynecologists!"

I waited until the air had cleared.

"I really would like to take you to the dance."

She looked up and gradually her expression softened. "You're a nice boy, and Shirley is a fool."

"I don't know about that. I don't have a date, and she's going out with a moderately wealthy, curly-headed quarterback. A lot of people would call me the fool."

Mrs. Butts didn't hear me, deep in her own thoughts. "I've really got to go. Mrs. Appel is waiting for me. You stay here and finish your coffee."

Of course I didn't. As soon as she stepped into the elevator, I hobbled up the stairs. We met again at Mrs. Appel's door.

"I'm serious about taking you to Round-up. You wouldn't have to dance with me or anything — I just think you need to get out."

She held the door open. "My daughter calls me a romantic, among other things, and I guess she's right. Why did you come to the hospital, Bubber? You came to ask me for a date, didn't you?"

I stuffed my hands in my pockets, looked down at my toes, and thought. If I told Mrs. Butts that, waiting for her, I had wrestled my tiger and got hurt, she might feel guilty enough to go out with me. This was one of the few times in my experience with women that the truth could get me what I wanted.

I looked up and lied, "Yes, ma'am, that's why I came to the hospital. To ask you out."

She smiled and touched my shoulder. "I'm flattered, I really am, but the answer is no. You stick with girls your own age; you'll have fewer problems that way."

Thinking of Shirley, I disagreed, but I disagreed silently.

"You go back to school now — your lunch break must be nearly over — and standing around here you're liable to catch an infection. I don't want that on my conscience." She pushed open the door and stepped inside, hesitating again. "But come visit me whenever you like. I enjoy talking to you."

As the door swung slowly shut I caught a glimpse of Mrs. Appel. The room was now full of soldiers, and Mrs.

Appel's gurney had been pushed into a corner, where she lay with her eyes half open. Slowly regaining consciousness, she gazed up at the perforated ceiling tiles as though they were distant stars, and listened to the moans around her in the fog of ether. She seemed to be testing her sensations. Was she dead? Was this The Other Side? *Which* Other Side? When she heard Mrs. Butts calling her name, she seemed to rise toward the words as though they were the first words she had ever heard spoken. And clasping Mrs. Butts's freckled arm, she felt warmth, and understood she was still alive. Or at least that was how it seemed to me.

Chapter
4

I WAS FALLING IN LOVE. I KNEW IT AS CER-
tainly as if I'd been bitten by Henry, our muscular timber
rattler. I was not certain, however, how to handle it. If
Mrs. Butts were one of those middle-aged women I'd read
about — downtrodden, deceiving, lazy, horny — I'd have
a chance with her; but if she *were* those things, I wouldn't
have wanted my chance. As it was, she had good character, which meant my chances were bad. Failure was not a
foregone conclusion, though.

On the way to Merry High I pondered deeply over this,
and when I ponder deeply I resemble the victim of food
poisoning. Or so Shirley informed me when I flopped
down at her snack bar table.

"If you're going to throw up, sit somewhere else," she
said, gnawing on a double cheeseburger. For a little girl,
Shirley had a fierce appetite.

"I'm not sick," I said, "but I just got twenty-three
stitches. Here, take a look."

Why I thought she'd want to see, I don't know.

"Ugh! *Not* while I'm eating," she said. "You really are

perverted." She paused to dip a french fry in some catsup, then languidly ate it. She wore a wooden bracelet that kept sliding up and down her arm. She shook her long hair and gave me an amused look.

"What's so funny?"

"You. Look at yourself. Wearing that Merry Tigers T-shirt and jeans for a change. And what'd you do this morning, stir your hair?"

I ran a hand over my head. My cowlick stuck up as usual, but to keep it down I'd have to stack bricks on it all night. Shirley went on looking amused.

"It's all over school, you know, about Momma catching us last night. What'd you say to her anyway?"

"Why?"

"Because she just came in, turned off the TV, and went to bed humming. No shouting or epileptic fits. And *why* are you grinning?"

"Oh, no reason. I guess I'm just a happy young man."

Mrs. Butts's weird behavior perked me up a little, and I began to feel hungry again. I bought five cheeseburgers and two strawberry malts, and carrying them back to the table I ran into Randy. He was leaning over Penny Budlacek's chair, sighting down her taut neck tendons to her bosoms. Penny had worn sleeveless blouses and false eyelashes ever since she'd decided to become an actress, in fifth grade, and she'd earned a bad reputation and a certain amount of appeal. I'd even dated her myself.

"Oh, Bubber!" she exclaimed, extending me her long, dramatic arm. "Randy just told me you got caught with your pants down. You must be picking up things from him."

47

"Randy's a well-known liar," I said, giving Penny her arm back. "I better take him away from you before he taints your mind."

"Just one moment," Penny uttered. She believed that actresses either uttered or exclaimed everything they said. "I was telling him about my big sister, Marty. She came home from San Jacinto State last week, with the crabs. She says she caught them from the dorm kitten — and Daddy believes her. Do you boys think that's possible?"

Randy cleared his throat. "I expect your daddy would believe most anything. At least I hope he does."

Penny smiled a wide, loose smile and took a big lick of her frogurt cone. I had to pull Randy off her like a leech, and he was still walking backwards when we stopped, halfway to Shirley's table. Good-looking, ready girls always made Randy want to comb his hair, and he dipped in his back pocket for a comb. But Randy was also the sort of fellow who lost things when sex was in the air.

"Hey, buddy, lend me yours."

"I don't use a comb; I stir my hair. Now come on, you've got to meet Shirley."

Randy was still staring enviously at Penny's frogurt. "Can't you take no for an answer? I told you last night on the phone, I'm not taking her out. She's got big friends and a bad temper. Now if you'll excuse me, I'm gonna go taint Penny in the parking lot."

Randy had disgraced his girlfriend Babs in a similar manner, in the parking lot. But he'd been so preoccupied with sex on that afternoon that he'd temporarily lost his car. They'd used Mr. Glaze's, the vice-principal, which surprised the ex-Marine when he came out early to drive to a school board meeting. Being interrupted by a red-faced ex-Marine would have made most boys more cautious.

"Get a grip on your hormones," I told him. "No more sex at school."

"But Penny's ready," he protested.

"So are the crabs," I said. "They're probably eating the whole family alive." I spoke softly, but nearby two lanky basketball players heard me. Penny? Crabs? They hit each other with their elbows and went off to spread the story.

Randy was a fussy dresser, the son of the clothing store owner in town. The possibility of crabs disturbed him. He hitched up his plaid Haggar slacks and looked over at Shirley. She was brushing her long blond hair, holding the wooden bracelet in her teeth.

"Okay. But if you weren't my offensive guard I wouldn't do it. Just remember: I didn't sneak around behind your back."

"I know, now come on. You two are really going to hit it off."

For once my prediction proved true. Shirley liked Randy for his curly-headed obsession with her body, and he liked her because she was willing and wasn't infested. By the time I'd finished my burgers they'd screwed up their eyes at mutual hatreds — parents, teachers, and sheriff's deputies, all of whom made having sex difficult — and had moved on to criticizing their hometown. It was flat and dead, unlike the swinging city where mixed drinks were served. The Houston Cadillac Club was of particular interest; two customers had recently shot each other in a dispute over a woman, and the club had

49

acquired a romantic reputation. Shirley actually became sweet when Randy opened his wallet to produce a club membership card, amid several brands of prophylactics.

"My brother Herb got it for me. He plays for the Cowboys, you know."

"Oh, wow," said little Shirley, touching the embossed letters on the card. A new range of experience seemed at her feet. When I left them she was talking in a husky voice, sliding the bracelet up and down her arm, and Randy seemed hypnotized.

But later, in the weight room after school, he seemed worried, sitting down on my bench pressing bench. I was staring at my thumbs, imagining the muscles of Mrs. Butts's arms locked around me.

"Earth calling Bubber, Earth calling Bubber, come in please."

"What?" I asked, irritated.

"I," Randy began, "I don't want me stealing Shirley to make you mad. I know you're pretty old-fashioned." I said nothing, and Randy cleared his throat. "I mean, up at the university you'll still be playing my side of the line, won't you?"

Randy was not a particularly brave quarterback, very timid about being tackled. Sometimes when a linebacker broke through, he'd drop the ball or point to the boy running with it. In one game he'd done it so often that Coach House, a good man, had swallowed his whistle and had to be carried off the field. But thanks to his older brother and his high-pressure, gung-ho father, Randy had gotten an undeserved scholarship. It was an ugly story, about a pushy family getting its way, and to everyone on the team but himself, Randy was a first-class loser. College football would eat him alive; he just didn't have the character to cut it. Strangely, though, it was his lack of character that made me like him most.

"Sure," I said, "don't worry. I won't let those college boys stomp you." I paused a moment, to let his relief set in. "So, you're taking Shirley out tonight, too?"

"Yeah. Why?"

"No reason." I lay back on the bench and started to work. While I pumped out twenty repetitions with two-eighty, Randy safe-checked me. Then he went off to complete his own workout. This consisted only of skipping rope in front of the big wall mirror. Randy was about as vain as he was oversexed. Once, when the crowd at Regionals had roared, I'd heard Randy shouting his own name, loud, just to hear the sound of it shouted. He imagined a glorious gridiron future for himself, much like his brother had had. A slot on the Cowboys, and a penthouse apartment full of plump pillows and scantily clad women. All he had to do was avoid getting tackled.

I could sure understand why Randy and Shirley hated our town. Driving through it that night I looked around. It was populated mainly by old folks, too poor or too stubborn to follow the young folks to jobs in the city. The streets were littered with wind-combed rice hulls and lumps of dung from the cattle trucks; the few banks in town were small; and there were only enough other businesses to keep the people fed, clothed, and drunk when they needed to be.

But drab and rural as Merry was, I admit I liked it. The

soil was rich, the people were fairly friendly, and from the overpass on the Interstate the distant, scattered ranchyard lights seemed in proper place with the big prairie stars. Younger people here, however, regularly went stir crazy.

I reached Mrs. Butts's house on the outskirts of town about an hour after Randy picked up Shirley. Coasting around back, out of sight of her curious next-door neighbors, my heart knocked and my big ears sweated. But I wasn't the only one hiding my car back there. A yellow Japanese sports car sat under the sumac trees beside Mrs. Butts's Pinto. I got out of my De Soto eyeing the house suspiciously. There didn't seem to be enough lights turned on inside, and through the kitchen door I thought I heard strange music.

When I walked around front I happened to look in the parlor window. Actually, I had to stand in the forsythia bushes and press my eye to the crack at the bottom of the windowshade. It was drawn down tonight. Something strange was going on inside. The naugehyde arm of Mrs. Butts's La-Z-Boy was lit with vast amounts of candlelight, and pressing my ear to the glass I heard the faint strains of a delicate Oriental music. Fascinated, I was still listening to it when Mrs. Butts leaned out the screen door and laughed.

"Bubber! I saw your ear under the blinds. It scared me."

I jumped back out of the forsythias and tried to act normal. This involved a lot of brushing at the wrinkles in my shirt sleeves. The shirt was new, from my college wardrobe, but I didn't want Mrs. Butts to think I'd worn a new shirt for her. She was obviously busy seducing a man. She wore a black, full-length kimono with a slit up the leg.

"Sorry to disturb you. I came to see Shirley, I guess — she's not here?"

Her green eyes sparkling, Mrs. Butts leaned on the door jamb and wrapped an arm around her waist. She enjoyed catching me in embarrassing predicaments.

"No, she's not here. But I'll tell her you were window-peeping for her." Then she added in a softer voice. "But you weren't peeping for her, were you?"

I pretended I didn't know what she meant, and looked at my toes. After a brief hesitation she stepped out and closed the door. "Come on up here. I give great advice to the lovelorn. And besides, it's a nice night to sit on the porch."

It was a nice night, cooler than before, and the Glad bags had been removed from the porch. The bosoms of Mrs. Butts's kimono were embroidered with lavendar dragons. But I climbed the steps reluctantly.

"I thought you were, ah, entertaining." I nodded at the door.

She touched a shell comb in her hair. "Thank you for thinking that, but I'm just entertaining myself." She paused. An explanation for her costume seemed in order. "Sometimes I give myself an Oriental Night — you know, cook chow mein and eat with chopsticks on the floor. It keeps me out of the doldrums of middle-age."

As she spoke she licked her fingers and twisted off the overhead porch bulb. Then she walked over to the porch rail using tiny, kimono-length steps. Apparently on Oriental Nights she pretended to *be* Oriental, too, and I found myself following in equally short steps. I must have looked like a Mongolian Idiot, but Mrs. Butts was gracious enough not to notice. She sat on the porch rail and patted a spot for me, not to close but close enough that I could smell her breath. It smelled of rice, like the prairie — or like the sake wine she was drinking.

For the next several minutes, while our eyes adjusted to the starlight, we sat comfortably silent. The prairie breeze was picking up, smelling of rain. Mrs. Butts leaned back on one arm and sipped sake from a cup. I glanced casually at her dragons.

"You really aren't middle-aged," I said. "You can't be much over thirty."

She smiled. "I'm thirty-five — and an *old* thirty-five after a day like today."

"Then you really are at your peak." She looked at me — *which* peak? I added quickly, "For marathon running. All you need is some exercise."

"Like dancing?" She smiled again. "Shirley said you were awfully good at it."

"Yes, ma'am, I am. Mom made me take four years of Cotillion; she thought that a big boy should have some grace." I paused. "What else did Shirley tell you?"

She covered a deeper smile with her sake cup, but she couldn't cover the amusement in her eyes. "She said you once let her jump on your stomach, from a chair."

"Only once," I defended, "and it was a very low chair. I wanted to show her she couldn't hurt me."

Mrs. Butts shook her hair — she had mounds of it — and laughed. "That's the wrong way, Bubber. Besides, she said she'd stepped on tougher tubes of tooth-paste."

I laughed along with her. "Yeah, I guess I've got two left feet with women."

Mrs. Butts found that funny, too. She gave my knee a friendly pat. "That's all right; I wouldn't enjoy you so much with different feet. I learned all about lady-killers from my ex."

We quieted down — I guess the mention of her ex-husband did it. Too bad, because it took Mrs. Butts's mind off me. She seemed to enjoy talking to me. I sucked in my breath and looked over at her. "Just the same, I don't think you should give up on us male animals entirely. You really ought to get out."

"You're so persistent," she said, smiling. "You remind me of some stubborn horses my dad owned. But you lied to me today, didn't you? Nancy Walker's a friend of mine; she mentioned a strange case in emergency."

Before I could answer she hopped off the rail. "Come on, I want to see those stitches in the light. Dr. Frank is also known as Frankenstein."

I followed her inside. If Mrs. Butts wasn't entertaining, she should have been. Her parlor, heavily forested with potted philodendrons, was lit by twenty jade green candles burning savagely in an enormous brass candela-bra. From a large bookshelf in the corner a record player played Oriental music. The atmosphere had the air of romance, and fantasy. Had I stumbled onto Mrs. Butts's pet frivolity?

Slightly embarrassed, she blew out the candles, turned

on a floor lamp, and explained: "On Oriental Nights I go whole hog." She couldn't bring herself to turn off the music, so she opened the windowshade, which altered the atmosphere considerably. All business now, she came back from the bathroom with a squeeze bottle of Phisohex soap and a towel, and motioned me from her shelves and shelves of books over to her recliner. I sat on the arm with my boot off and my naked, hairy leg in her lap. She examined the stitches and tenderly washed the skin.

"Maybe you could use a cup of sake," she said, mopping up. "This must have been painful."

"It was." Gradually I had been slipping over the arm of her chair, into the seat. The slit in Mrs. Butts's kimono had come open; vast sections of her legs were freckled, and those legs were fuzzy, too. Mrs. Butts didn't shave! What legs! I kept talking and slipping over.

"Terribly, terribly painful. But no thanks on the liquor. Shirley got me drunk once — she probably told you — I went crazy and ate the Dixie cup. But no one in my family can drink sanely. My grandfather rode his mule home from the saloon one night, into a tree. The mule lived, but grandpa and the tree died."

Mrs. Butts caught herself smiling. "I'm sorry — about your grandfather, I mean. It's a funny story, though."

"That's okay, but now I've got a question for you. Who belongs to that yellow car out back?"

"Oh," she said. "Oh, that's Shirley's. A birthday present from her father." Then she added with some pleasure, "The engine exploded the first day."

Her obvious pleasure embarrassed her, so she looked

around for something else to say. Noticing I was fully in the chair, she gave me a playful shove.

"You're just like my own grandpa's bluetick hound. First one paw on the chair, and the next thing he was snoring in your lap."

"I'm persistent like a coon dog," I admitted, "and I want you to know, I'm an early bloomer, very mature for my age. Look: I've already got hair in my ears." I put my arm around her and my ear to her eye.

She laughed softly. "I'm sure you're *not* like the other boys." Then she grew nervously silent. She was sitting in a chair with a boy who wanted a kiss. I don't think this had happened to her in some time. To avoid my expectant eyes she looked at my hairy leg. In particular she looked at the spot where my boot top had rubbed the hair away; boot-baldness seemed a fact about men she'd forgotten. She absently touched my skin. We sat a moment longer, listening to each other's breath. The only thing that prevented me from kissing her was a lack of courage. The Oriental music sounded like a thin, romantic rain. She breathed; it rained; I waited.

Gradually, though, another sound crept into our consciousness: the sound of Randy's Bonneville convertible, coasting into spying position outside.

Like armadillos on the highway, we put out heads down and froze. A terrible scene was coming and we'd need all our strength. Besides, we were immovably wedged, hip to hip in the deep recliner. Mrs. Butts did manage to roll down my jeans, but we couldn't reach my boot on the floor.

Shirley could just see the tops of our heads but she didn't waste any time pulling Randy out of the car. As they stormed up the porch steps she told him, "If this man gives us any trouble, I want you to hit him. You'll do that for me, won't you — after what I did for you?"

Randy mumbled a noncommittal reply. He wanted to see how large this man was before he made any promises.

When they burst in the screen door I raised my face. I'd never seen Shirley's jaw drop so quickly. "You!" She stabbed me with her eyes. "*You!*" She bludgeoned her mother.

"Yes," Mrs. Butts said calmly. "You came home right on cue. Now run go call your father — tell him I'm misbehaving. This is your big chance."

"Don't" — Shirley shook her little fist — "you mention Daddy when you're arm in arm with *my* ex-boyfriend. I *knew* you'd start this!"

She wore a small madras sundress with a scooped neckline that revealed the propped-up tops of her bosoms. They were scarlet with anger. She wanted to kill us both, but she lacked the weapon; Randy stood sheepishly behind her, measuring the distance to the door. Shirley glared at my boot on the carpet, my arm around her mother.

I attempted to explain. "Your mom was just examining my stitches."

Little Shirley smirked as if to say, Don't lie to me. Her smirks resembled a bee sting. Then she stamped her foot and turned to Randy.

"Hit him! In the *groin!*"

Randy blinked. "My offensive guard? No thanks. I'll just go put the top up on my car."

He made a move to leave but Shirley caught his arm. "If you *don't* hit him, our date's off for tomorrow. And remember what I promised?"

Randy looked back at me. He valued his offensive guard, but Shirley must have promised him worlds. The moment hung on his decision. He took his hands out of his pockets; Mrs. Butts interrupted.

"Nobody's getting hit in *my* house. Now Shirley, *you* go to your room." As she spoke she attempted to unwedge herself from the chair, which involved some pushing and shoving on my body. The sight of her touching my thighs didn't soothe Shirley.

"I hate you!" she hollered. At a loss she added, "And I *hate* Chinese music!" She flew over to the bookshelf, jerked the record loudly off the player, and hurled it at us. We were having a tough time getting up, but fear motivated us. Unfortunately our fear also motivated something in Shirley. Hysteria. She looked around and started hurling books at us. Within seconds she was throwing them like a well-oiled book-throwing machine. Randy got conked by a recent best-seller, and he dropped straight to the carpet holding his nose. Mrs. Butts and I managed to dive behind her sheltering chair.

As I say, being with Shirley was often like being in a war. A cannonade of romance novels bombarded us, followed by a barrage of nonfiction hardbacks. Then the volley slowed as Shirley's accuracy improved. We were regularly struck on the head and shoulders. From time to time Shirley hollered indiscriminately, *"I h a t e y o u!"*

"She's got our range," I said, hugging onto Mrs. Butts. She was grinning like a sergeant in a foxhole.

"I think it's time for you to leave," she said, "while she's still throwing light comedies. The Britannicas are next, and they're heavy."

"You'll be all right?"

She patted my arm. "I'm having fun. Now, go!"

At a run I scooped up Randy, who was semiconscious, and dragged him outside. Not more than four medium-sized novels hit me in the crown. But the pain was worth it because Shirley became too distracted to throw well at her mother, who ran in a low crouch down the hall to her bedroom.

Outside, to the east over Fort Bend County, flat-bottomed thunderheads were blowing in, and a refreshing breeze spilled down as I helped Randy to his car. We stood a moment, cooling off and coming back to our senses.

"Damn, that smarts." He touched his nose. "Is it gonna swell?"

"No," I said, brushing yard dirt off my bootless foot. "And I'm real sorry about all this."

"You ought to be. If it wasn't for you I'd be undressing Shirley right now. Help me put the top up on this thing, before it starts to rain."

After Randy drove off I hopped around back of the house to my car. Through the kitchen window I could see Shirley talking on the phone. "That's right, she's gone sex-crazy. I told you she was a bad influence, Daddy. . . .

What's the matter? Who's there? Are you entertaining cattle buyers again?"

I hopped up to Shirley's yellow Datsun and kicked its rear tire with my booted foot.

"Kick my car twice," said Mrs. Butts, from my front seat.

When I stopped jumping up and down in fright, she said, "You'd better get in before it rains." She sat in the center of the front seat wearing her kangaroo robe again. She held my boot on her lap. I slid in beside her.

"I've always loved the smell of these old cars," she said. "My brother had one like this. And that armadillo in the back reminds me of a chaperone I once had."

She paused and we watched the distant lightning spitting down from the thunderheads. They were sweeping into Waller County now, and a gusty, moist wind rattled the backyard sumacs.

"Shirley's real mad," I said. "I'm sorry about that."

"She's always mad at me. I expect she'll convince her dad to keep her this summer."

"That'll make her happy."

Mrs. Butts smiled. "I doubt it. She has a lot of fantasies about living with him — none of them true."

"I guess it's that way with fantasies," I said.

She smiled again, more thoughtfully. "Oh, I don't know. Sometimes fantasies almost suffice."

We seemed on the verge of having a distracting, intelligent conversation, and we didn't want to fall into that. Mrs. Butts had come out here to get kissed, and I ached to oblige her. All we had to do was find a way for the fireworks to begin, naturally.

We spent a quiet moment thinking under the thunder-filled sky, and then I began to lean toward her. I toppled slowly, a collapsing tower of Pisa, letting gravity bring us closer. First out shoulders bumped, then our heads. Touching hers, Mrs. Butts turned to say "ouch!" but I plugged her lips with my mouth. It was a messy first kiss. She didn't respond, but she didn't resist either. I drew back to let her breathe.

"I must be crazy," she said.

"You're the most beautiful woman in the world," I replied.

"*You* must be crazy," she said. But my sincerity seemed to have touched her. "If you're going to say things like that," she added, "you ought to call me Rose."

"All right, Rose." My voice cracked slightly with emotion, which made her smile. For some reason I'd slumped in my seat and was eye-level with her mouth. "I want you to know I'm nineteen; I got set back a year in third grade. Now can I kiss you again? I really enjoyed it."

"Bubber, I don't think—"

"You might as well," I went on; "you're getting blamed for it on the phone right now."

At first she seemed unfamiliar with kissing, but within a few minutes Mrs. Butts (Rose) was rising to my lips just as Mrs. Appel had risen to the sound of her name. Oddly, though, we both kept our hands in our laps, so just our mouths touched. But at the first drumming of the rain on the De Soto roof, Rose slid out and bent down at the door. I loved the way her robe opened.

"I can't let you take me to the dance," she said. "But I'll

probably see you there. I think you're right about getting out." Then, closing the car door firmly, she ran barefooted across the puddling backyard and climbed into her bedroom window. Shirley was still in the kitchen, dialing a new number on the telephone.

Chapter
5

THE ELECTRICAL STORM LEFT MERRY FEELING thoroughly washed and highly charged, and the next morning the men in town went off to their jobs cheerfully certain that tonight they'd get falling down drunk. None of the petty workaday irritations could ruffle them, not on Round-up day.

In the afternoon the women of town left their beauty parlors to do their last-minute Piggly Wiggly shopping and I saw scores of them in the frozen food aisle, my usual haunt. One breezy older lady saw me, too, and marched down the aisle giving advice. I didn't recognize her with her hair done up, but she could have been one of a dozen breezy older ladies who'd adopted me after Mom died.

"Bubber! Oh, Bubber!" she sang out. I was trying to hide behind the L'Eggs display. "Are you shopping for your daddy's supper?"

I had four Hungry Man dinners in my hand. "No, ma'am. Dad cooks mainly for his colon, and I'm a little young for that."

"Well, colon or no colon, you be sure to get some pot pies down him before tonight. Nothing's worse for a man his age than getting drunk and throwing up empty. My own daddy, bless his soul, upchucked himself to death on Texas Independence Day. State holidays," she sighed, "they take such a toll on the family."

I didn't get a chance to feed Dad, though. All afternoon while I tried to dry out the De Soto's waterlogged spark wires, he and Sinclair sat inside among the snakes, staring at a fresh bottle of Jim Beam. At their age they couldn't afford to drink much of it, they knew, but they wanted to very much. When I finally came inside, wiping my greasy hands on my jeans, they appeared to be deep in worship.

"Car fixed?" Dad asked, his eyes on the bottle.

"No. I'm afraid I'll have to ride with Sinclair. Did you decide to risk it, too, Charlie?"

Sinclair gave me a wink and Dad cleared his throat. He didn't know how to admit he wanted to dance with a woman again.

"I guess I better go. Sinclair would kill himself driving with Mr. Jim Beam."

"Okay, but remember you two: No drinking while you're driving. My young life is at stake."

Both of them nodded dumbly, though they had every intention of breaking their promise. About an hour before we left, Sinclair brought in a plastic cleaner's bag full of their best clothes freshly pressed. Sinclair wore his red boots with the white star of Texas on the toes, and the turquoise nugget on Dad's string tie caught the light like a fishing lure. Sinclair then, in a ceremony of sorts, broke the crisp paper seal on the Jim Beam and poured four or five inches each into some grape jelly glasses. He winked across the kitchen at me.

"Better get dressed, Bubber. My truck don't wait for no man, not when it's headed toward women."

"Ladies," Dad corrected, and turned his attention back to the sour mash. It was ludicrous, the way those two old boys felt about liquor, but it seemed to make them feel young.

And all their youth did was cause trouble. On the drive to pick up Claudine and her brown-eyed friend Lucy Taylor, the old fellows bounced over two mailboxes, then lost control and hit the doghouse in Reverend Sunday's backyard. The last I saw of the dog, he was dragging his chain and biting after a pedestrian.

I wish I could say their dates were a couple of calm old ladies, but Lucy Taylor was a goodtime Texas gal from way back and Claudine was nothing but Bohemian. They hopped into the front seat, Lucy Taylor hollering, "Drive fast, boys, but don't hit no cats. I like cats." I may have blacked out for part of the journey — when they bounced off the tree and mowed down the mortician's picket fence — but I definitely remember the dancehall parking lot.

They spun into the oyster shell parking lot at about fifty miles an hour and nearly ran over a fistfight in progress. The fighters dove for cover as Sinclair fishtailed past, with Dad's help, and plowed into a chain link fence. Steel poles bent, mesh wire sang, and the four passengers up front whooped and hooted like kids on a roller coaster. By the time the fence slingshot us backward, the fistfighting boys had found where they'd laid down their wristwatches and were running to the dancehall for their lives.

Dad stumbled out of the cab and held the door open for the ladies. They were all laughing, the common fear of the journey having made them fast friends.

"Durn it, Sinclair. I didn't think this old truck could still punch holes in a hurricane fence."

Sinclair proudly smited his dented hood. "I told you, this automobile has *umph!*"

"Well, you two hell-raisers put your teeth back in and let's go dance." Claudine was speaking. When her second mean husband had died, she'd worked his cattle leases until they expired. Then she'd needed work indoors, at sixty-six, and took a job in a beer joint. A good-laughing woman, she still knew when to be strict with men. "From now on we're going to have fun that's legal."

Sinclair let out a disappointed Bohemian hoot, Lucy Taylor squealed, Dad offered Claudine his arm, and they all stepped lightly inside.

I'd been riding in the truckbed and my step wasn't so light. I was partially buried in pieces of picket fence. Brushing myself off I limped to the dancehall door, where I stopped to look for Rose and sniff my dirty clothes.

Round-up was sponsored by the Mexican Roping Club and the American Legion, and there was already a lively crowd. Cowboys, rice farmers, and rednecks lined the Legion Hall bar, hugging coiffed women and waving dollar bills for drinks. And at the edge of the dance floor well-groomed rogue males and a squad of bandaged soldiers chased coveys of unescorted, laughing girls. The dance floor was jammed, too, with young people hopping up and down and older folks gliding in between them. The Burly Boys Band was playing and they were good.

I didn't see Rose, but behind me, in the darkness behind the door, I heard a woman slapping a man repeatedly.

"Damn, Lucille, why'd you do that for?"

"Flies," she said, a little drunk. "You had flies all over your face."

The fella rubbed his jaw. "Well I wished you'd hit 'em softer. You could accidentally sober me up."

Shirley, with her keen eyesight and keener desire to foul things up, spotted me from across the Legion Hall and dragged her date over. Randy hadn't hit my groin, so she'd gone out with the school hoodlum instead. Tyronne, better known as Tire-iron, only came to school occasionally, to beat up a teacher or two and blow his nose on the books. I nodded hello and he gave me a tiny-eyed, drunken smirk. He thought he'd stolen my girl. He was built like a mountain, with the smallest part on top.

"You're early," Shirley said, "and your clothes are dirty. My mother's not here yet."

"Oh?"

Shirley smiled in a way that made me sick. "No, she went over to a doctor's apartment first. They're having a party — a Highball Primer. She's wearing her diaphragm, too. I showed Tyronne the empty case, didn't I?"

Tire-iron didn't hear. He was gazing down at Shirley's wavy blond hair with the tiny eyes and great tenderness of a drunken bully.

"That's good," I said, feeling hot in the chest. "I'm glad she's getting out."

68

I tried to walk away as though I had not been stabbed, but found I needed to sit down. The nearest table was filled with younger fellows from school. They were drinking bourbon from under the table and talking about the usual things: screwing every girl on the dance floor.

"You know what I'd do with her, I'd —"

"You couldn't, not with that little pencil you've got. Now me, I'm hung like a horse."

"Good, if you have a date with a horse. I'm talking about girls, though."

"No, you're not," Bob Dallas said. He was an older black guy who hung out with younger boys because he was ugly. A knotty nose, chipped teeth in front, and a haircut his poor mother had given him. But a very tough linebacker. "You pissants are talking about your third legs. That's the difference between pissants and seniors. Me and Bubber here, *we* talk about women."

Everybody turned their attention back to a nearby covey of girls and strained to talk only about them. Sometimes, at that age, we could imagine screwing a girl so intensely that it actually seemed to happen. The temperature above our table must have risen, and the covey seemed to feel our heat. I saw Penny Budlacek flap her false eyelashes at me. But I was in no condition to flap back. It seemed that I'd lit Mrs. Butts's fire, only to have some doctor get warm by it.

Randy sat down with us then and noticed where we were ogling. "Hey, you guys want some of that? Come on, we'll drag a few of them out to the parking lot. Nothing's too good for my offensive line."

He clapped me sincerely on the shoulder. Randy might

have been timid about the opposing line, but he'd wade right into the opposite sex. The loss of Shirley hadn't affected him either. Like the other rogues he wore loud lizard skin boots, and the pearlized shirt buttons were unsnapped down his chest.

But his gracious offer made the younger boys nervous. "Naw," said little Johnny Boni. "The soldiers already got the easy ones, except for Penny and she's got the crabs. Let's just go drive fast in your car."

Johnny Boni didn't have a car of his own and he'd ride anywhere with anyone, as long as they drove too fast. He got his chance a little later when the bottle under the table ran out and the guys got up to make a liquor run. Bob Dallas usually bought it, because he had a method. He wore an eyepatch and limped; the cashiers always sold liquor to ugly, underaged cripples.

After they left Randy slipped out to the parking lot with Sondra Nickle, a gullible little brunette from a broken home, and I moved over to mope on an empty beer keg. The Burly Boys were playing a lively polka for the old folks, and I saw Dad sailing the floor with Claudine. He hadn't danced with a woman since Mom died, but he hadn't forgotten how. I'd never seen an old man move his feet so fast. Nearby Sinclair was waltzing Lucy Taylor at a more reasonable speed, while feeling up her ample rump. She had bursitis there, he claimed.

When the tune ended Dad and Claudine couldn't stop. They set sail for my beer keg. Dad could tell I felt blue and tried to help.

"I didn't pay for Cotillion so you could plaster the walls. Get out here and show us how."

"My leg," I explained. "Stitches."

"Durn your leg," he said. "If that tiger didn't drain you, you still got some of my blood. Pick yourself a partner and don't step on her too much."

Claudine pitched in, too. "Better do what Charlie says. This old mule's a dancing fool." She was following Dad's lead and loving it.

Really, I preferred good dancing to moping, so I went over to the covey and flushed out Penny. The rumor I'd started about her infested family had spread and no other fellows would come near her.

"If you dance with me, I won't bloody your feet."

"Oh, Bubber," she uttered. "You say the strangest things."

The band was playing a country waltz and we did the Cotton Eyed Joe around the floor. This dance is performed with the woman's hands hooked into the man's belt loops, while his right hand chokes her neck. Sometimes when the fellow got too excited, he choked too hard and the woman yelped; but I tried to be gentle with Penny.

She was a good-looking girl with creamy arms and honey-colored hair, and while we danced we had a good-natured argument about California. I warned her that it was full of fast-talk artists, drug addicts, and roller-skaters who primal-screamed. Penny just laughed; she came from a large Catholic family — a grocer and a swaybacked wife with eight or nine kids — and compared to that, California didn't seem too bad. Still, I had to warn her that honey-colored girls from Merry, Texas, were the film moguls' lunches out there. "Stay here, please. You don't want to go some place where people Rolf, do you? And don't laugh; I'm worried about you." Penny seemed a little touched by that, but she told me not to worry; she had strong bones under her creamy skin. We waltzed a little longer, in a friendly affectionate way. Penny was an extremely graceful dancer.

But rubbernecking the dancehall for Rose was made difficult by Penny's hairdo. It was a bubblehead cut and hard to peer around. Still, I did manage to spot Rose the minute she came in. She wore a royal purple, string-shouldered dress, and with her green eyes and red hair she looked as pretty as a prairie flower. But flowers attract bugs and she was surrounded by them: young doctors. Dr. Shorts, the gynecologist, guided her and Nurse Walker to a table in the rear, his hand on the small of Rose's back.

"Ouch," Penny said. "You're squeezing my neck awful hard."

"I'm sorry. What were you saying?"

"I was telling you not to worry. Marty and I sleep in different rooms, and I spray the toilet bowl with Lysol."

"If you say so," I said, giving her neck a little squeeze. I felt bad, ignoring her. "But I'm already starting to itch."

"Oh, you!" Penny tugged at my belt loops. "You just love to tease the girls. Who was that you were staring at?"

"Mrs. Butts, Shirley's mother."

"Uh-ho, that's one girl I wouldn't make mad. But before you run off, dance another number with me without scratching. Maybe then the other boys won't be so scared."

Of course, I did; I felt responsible for her isolation. I even made her laugh with the story about the tick that got stuck in my eyelashes. Soon, the hungry rogues on the sidelines got courage to face the crabs, and a fellow with a large hat cut in on us.

I headed straight for Rose. The men at her table seemed to lean over her purple dress. Could doctors sense a woman wearing a diaphragm?

She saw me coming, said something to them, and met me on the edge of the dance floor. We looked at each other in a moment of silence, before she said, in a firm voice that meant bad news, "Bubber, I want to —"

"Dance with me?" I interrupted. "Delighted." I took her up and started moving my feet. "Holler when I step on you hard."

The Burly Boys were playing "Your Cheatin' Heart" and we danced close together. Oh my, her bare-shouldered body felt nice. Even her deltoids were freckled; they almost seemed hand-painted. I didn't do any fancy dips or spins because I wanted her to feel comfortable. But she didn't feel that way. Every time our thighs touched, her spine tensed up and we tripped. We bumped into each other often, too, and at one point we resembled two people trying to pass in a narrow hall. Apparently we had to talk before we could dance. I whispered into her ear: "If you don't relax, you'll get cramps and sweat heavily. What did you want to talk about?"

She drew back, smiling. "I wanted to apologize, for last night. I'm afraid I got carried away."

"Don't say another word. This big-eared boy enjoyed

73

himself." I pulled her close again and stuck my nose in her hair. "You look beautiful in that dress. I hope I'm not getting it dirty."

"Why, thank you," she said, momentarily flustered. "It's new." I could feel her grinning against my shoulder. "And you're not getting it dirty."

We danced some more, more comfortably. But when the set ended she led me a short way off the floor, where she avoided my eyes under the Legion's NATO flags.

"What I wanted to say was this: Last night was fine. We didn't do any permanent damage. But tonight . . ." She paused, I think because I was groaning. She smiled then, looked up, and punched me affectionately in the biceps.

"Stop making those awful throat noises. I feel guilty enough as it is, leading a nice boy on." Then she gave me a firm shove in the direction of the covey. "Just go enjoy yourself with a girl the right age."

Moments later I'd gotten a cup of fruit punch and had found my empty beer keg again. Rose's table seemed filled with degenerating doctors. It disgusted me, the way they looked at the nurses. All they had on their minds was sex — which was on my mind, too, but in a purer form. Rose wore sandals tonight.

A pouchy-eyed, proctologist-looking fellow drained his glass and asked Rose to dance. But on the floor the proctologist couldn't dance at all; he just laid his head on her shoulder and more or less went comatose. When Rose tried to stand him up straight, he nearly fell over backwards, so she let him rest on her until the song finally ended. It was a new ballad, "You Walked All Over My Heart, And Squashed That Sucker Flat."

Randy eased up to me then, retucking his shirttail and grinning so I'd know he scored. "Sondra says I look like Elvis when I sneer. Do I?"

Randy sneered.

"No, not at all. You look like you inhaled a bug."

I looked back at Rose ordering another drink. She didn't seem to be having much fun, but I guessed she preferred miserable company her own age. I tossed my punch cup behind a bale of hay.

"Come on, let's go get drunk. I know where there's a bottle hidden."

We went out across the oyster shell parking lot to Sinclair's truck, where I chugged about a quarter of the bottle before Randy wrestled it away. Inside, the Burly Boys played "Okie From Muskogee," and the hot crowd hooted.

"She's got you hooked, I can see that," Randy said, carefully wiping the lip of the bottle. "But if you want some advice, stay sober and hope she gets drunk. That way if she falls down, you won't miss when you jump on her."

Randy was bad company, but he was company. We sat on Sinclair's battered hood for a half-hour or more, listening to the music through the door and watching the couples sneaking out to their cars. The forlorn, broken-hearted country tunes seemed to stimulate their sex hormones, and from a nearby Ford pickup, where no heads were visible, we heard a girl say:

"Hush up and quit grunting. I want to hear the words to this song."

It was a good imitation of Waylon Jenning's latest,

75

which began "The only things that make Life worth livin'/are well-tuned guitars and firm-feeling women."

The girl in the Ford began to sob. "I'm sorry I stepped on your guitar, Larry. I didn't know it was setting on the floorboards."

"There, there, it's all right, Lucille. You was drunk and I shouldn't of brought it anyway. Now wiggle a little more, will you?"

Randy wanted to go peek in their truck window, but I dragged him back toward the dancehall. Halfway there we ran into Tire-iron. He had a nasty, drunken look in his eye, and a half-dozen sassy friends behind him. His nickname came from his habit of laying a tire-iron under his car each time he parked. If he went down in a fight, he could come up with something extra. I noticed he stopped beside his souped-up Chevy Malibu.

"Hey, Blubber Dumb," he hollered. "I want to speak to your ass."

"What did he say?" I asked Randy.

"I think you had enough sour mash. Come on."

I took another slug of Jim Beam before I handed it to Randy. Ordinarily I avoided fighting because I was bad at it, but I couldn't stand to be called that name. Blubber Dumb! Children had chanted it at me in grade school. I stomped up to Tire-iron. He wore an empty bottle of Boone's Farm stuck on his thumb.

"You owe me an apology," I said. "You might not have noticed, but I'm not fat and stupid anymore."

Tire-iron laughed. He was a big boy without being muscular, like a gorilla that lived near bananas. "You're a wise-ass, Blubber, you know that? A goddamned, motherfucking wise-ass. And you can't hold your liquor either."

He waggled the bottle in my face to emphasize his words, but he didn't need to do that. I was sobering up real fast, surrounded by his friends. Most of them smelled like they'd been lifting heavy machinery all day. I glanced back for Randy, but saw him slinking in the dancehall door. A person had to be seated before Randy considered hitting him. I looked back at Tire-iron's magnified thumb, and swallowed thoughtfully.

"Fine," I said. "I see your point. I'm a goddamned, motherfucking wise-ass. Anything else?"

Tire-iron considered a moment, his tiny eyes indicating thought. "You're a prevert, too. What the hell kind of man takes a girl out, then sneaks off with her momma?" He turned to his buddies. "Ain't that some kind of incest?"

"If it ain't, it should be," one offered.

"And it sure as hell pissed Shirley off, them two dancing together."

"Damn straight it did." Tire-iron wagged the bottle again. "My leg still hurts where she kicked me."

"I'm sorry," I said. "She should have kicked *me*. I'll go right in and let her do it now."

Tire-iron stopped me by taking a fistful of my shirt. "You stay away from Shirley, *and* her mother."

"Now wait a second," I said, getting mad. That was my shirt he was tearing, a shirt I planned to wear to college. "What's between me and Mrs. Butts is *not* you. And as for Shirley, she's just using you. She's probably already told you she's never been so happy in her life."

Tire-iron let loose of me and lowered the bottle. He

stared at me with a strange steadiness, as if he were staring from his pit of corruption into mine. What he felt for Shirley seemed fine and pure to him; my feelings didn't compare. He decided to hit me.

So I hit him first. I put everything I had into that punch — all my years of wrestling Bengal, lifting weights, tackling dummies. A looping roundhouse right to the cheek.

Tire-iron had bones there, unfair bones so hard that the gristle in my shoulder popped. His cheek bounced, but he didn't wince, or rock on his feet, or blink more than once.

Flipping the bottle away in an odd, chivalrous gesture — fine Shirley shouldn't be associated with a wine bottle murder — he put my head in his elbow and squeezed it. My eyes began to pop out.

"Twist his head off and shit down his lungs!" his happy friends shouted.

Where were *my* friends? Off getting liquor, I remembered.

"Stomp his fucking gourd!"

I flailed and kicked and even tried to pinch him, without much success. When he tired of crushing my skull, he started pounding it against the hood of his Chevy. I tried to pull the windshield wiper off and stab him with it, but one of his friends, who was standing on the hood to get a good view of my murder, jumped up and down on my hand. He wore workboots, I recall.

"Kick him in the nuts!" his friends hollered. "Kick his fucking nuts off!"

"Shit," Tire-iron said, throwing my body on the

ground. "I doubt he's got any nuts. Did he break my wiper blade?"

He momentarily forgot me, inspecting his wiper, and I began a cautious slow crawl toward the underbelly of his car. I had to protect myself; I groped in the oyster shell for his tire-iron.

But it wasn't there! Of course it wasn't, you fool! He wouldn't leave it there for anyone to use. Tire-iron was smarter than his legend.

I tried to crawl under his car.

Laughing, he pulled me out, jumped on my back, and rode me around the parking lot, steering by my ears.

"Pull them things off!" the crowd chanted. "Pull them ears off!"

Tire-iron began to pull off my ears.

Thinking that the rest of my life I'd have to explain how a boy named Tire-iron had peeled off my ears gave me strength. I stood up. Tire-iron slid off my back, holding onto one ear for a long second. Finally he let go and fell on his butt — and then good fortune struck. Falling, Tire-iron's head smacked down on the bumper, and with a groan he stretched out in the oyster shell.

It took his buddies a moment to conceive of their hero unconscious, before they came back to life. Someone punched me in the liver with his class ring. Someone hit me twice in the heart, and then someone kicked at my hip so hard that his loafer sailed away — high, over the roof of a car, and we all watched, stunned by its grace — and finally someone brought me down with thick knuckles to the thin nose. As I fell, the crisscrossed laces of a workboot caught my chin, and I tumbled head over heels in the oyster shell.

I lay very still, pretending to be dead. It wasn't a difficult acting job, since I wasn't sure myself. Somewhere out in the darkness I heard additional feet.

"Hey, what the hell?" Bob Dallas shouted. Without waiting for explanations, he hit the fellow with the workboots with the Old Forester, sending out a delicate cascade of broken glass and fresh bourbon. My other teammates jumped in, too, and soon everyone found someone to hit.

I lay on my back and watched for a while, and then I squirmed under Sinclair's truck. I didn't want anyone falling and hurting me. Hearing the commotion outside, the spirited men left their dance partners and poured out the door. Excited, they began hitting everyone they didn't know by the first name, even some soldiers in casts. I hoped no one was getting hurt seriously, but to check I'd have to stick my tender head out. One of my ears felt broken, and when I pulled the top of it, the ear came unsnapped, like my pajama snaps. I lay back self-piteously and watched the scuffling boots.

About the time everyone was getting tired, Deputy Dozel turned on his siren in the corner of the lot and fired his pistol in the air. "All right," he spoke into his bullhorn, "we had our Round-up fistfight. Now quit poking each other and get back inside."

Exhaustion made everyone obey. After the walking had limped away, the women came out to sort through the unfortunates crawling on the ground. I stayed out of sight under the truck; as far as I was concerned, I'd stay under the truck forever. Life was too dangerous elsewhere.

But a life passes slowly under a truck. I don't know how much time elapsed before Shirley's shoes appeared. They walked up to Tyronne's body, followed by Randy's loud boots. After a brief look at her newest ex-boyfriend, she climbed onto the hood of his Malibu and looked around.

"Bubber's not out here, and he's not inside. Maybe he crawled off in a ditch and died." Shirley's voice was full of satisfaction.

Meanwhile, Randy touched Tyronne's nose with his boot. "Damn, look how ugly he is, unconscious."

Shirley took another look. "Help me down, Ransom," she said sweetly. "And quit looking up my dress." On the ground she slipped her arm into his. He wasn't a fighter, but she didn't need one anymore. "It looks like I'm gonna need a ride home." She gave Randy's arm a suggestive squeeze. His sex hormones went off the chart.

"Sure, sure, I'll take you, but I think I lost my car. It's probably over in that direction." He started dragging Shirley into the bushes, but she remained in control.

"In a minute," she said. "First I really want to say goodbye to Momma."

Again, I don't know how long it took for Tyronne to regain consciousness. He got to his feet, rubbing his head and mumbling, then shuffled off. Another pair of shoes appeared next. Sandals. They stopped beside the truck and called out.

"Bubber?"

I rolled out under Rose's dress, which scared her a bit.

When she settled down she made me sit on Sinclair's tailgate as she examined my face. It was pretty banged up, I imagine; my ear felt like it was dangling. Rose's face was good medicine, though. She dabbed at the blood with the hem of her new dress.

"Don't," I said.

"Don't tell me what to do," she replied with authority. "I'm a trained nurse. Someone told me this fight started over me."

"Who said that?"

"Ransom — now quit squirming. I'm trying to assess the damage I caused."

I was quiet a moment, then said, "Don't believe Randy. He's a well-known liar."

"He wasn't lying when he told me you needed help. He saw your boot under the truck. Now hold *still*."

She was exceptionally tender with me, though everything she did hurt exceptionally. But I liked her face close to mine. She had a sufficient amount of whiskey on her breath. I began to rub her bare shoulder.

"Wouldn't you rather I got doctored by a girl my own age?"

"Be quiet," she said, then smiled. "A whole army of sixteen-year-olds couldn't keep up with your injuries."

She drove me home in her Pinto and got me upstairs. I took off my shirt and boots and slipped gratefully into bed.

"You weren't afraid of the snakes downstairs, were you? They're no more dangerous than doctors."

"I was petrified," she said, coming back from my

bathroom with a washcloth and adhesive. "I checked, but I didn't wet my pants. Now I'll have to bandage that ear. Some of the cartilage is torn."

"Okay." I made room for her on the bed. "But let it slump a little. I want a souvenir of tonight."

Rose smiled and sat down gingerly. My bed made her nervous; she looked around at my room. It was a small attic room, with books and magazines piled up against the short walls because I was too lazy to build bookcases. A pair of dumbbells lay on the floor beside an open copy of *Smithsonian*, and the only wall decorations were two prints, showing a man and a woman without skin. Labeled arrows were drawn to the various muscle groups. Mrs. Butts found that funny.

"I thought you'd at least have a poster of a girl in a wet T-shirt. Dr. Shorts did," she added, amused.

"Aw, I grew out of dirty posters when I stopped masturbating so much. Maybe Dr. Shorts hasn't stopped."

She laughed. "That's a thought," and I took the opportunity to sit up and kiss her. It was almost as good as last night. Better, considering that her shoulders were bare. She wore little gold earrings shaped like horseshoes, and somewhere a diaphragm.

"You lay back down," she said, but not firmly. I took her hand. We were breathing in each other's faces.

"My father won't be home until the last tune's played. We've got several hours yet."

"Don't say things like that. They make me nervous." She looked away.

"All right. But do me one favor."

"What?" she looked back, suspiciously.

"Go soak that dress in cold water. I'd feel terrible if I thought I'd bloodied it."

While she was in my bathroom, I shucked my jeans and faced the reading lamp into the wall. Then I lay down bathed in a mellow, romantic light, I hoped, and coughed so she'd know I was ready. After some time she came out, holding the limp wet dress against her chest. In the light coming up the stairs behind her, I could see her put a hand to her head. And I could hear her breathing.

"Bubber, I don't know what I'm doing."

"Don't worry," I said, "I do. I've read the Aggies' Sex Manual cover to cover."

The Texas Aggies, reputed to be the dumbest people in the state, were the brunt of most good jokes. I could feel Rose smiling across the room.

"And was the Sex Manual informative?"

"Oh, very. I memorized all three pages: Put in. Take out. Repeat, if necessary."

Laughing easily, she stepped up to my bed, still hidden behind the limp dress. "What am I going to do with you?"

Before I could answer what I hoped she'd do, she became dangerously serious again. "Really, Bubber, I don't know what I'm doing."

I answered her seriously for a change. "Neither one of us does, Rose. But take a chance and drop that dress. I'm anxious to start the Introduction."

Rose did drop the dress, and climbed under the covers quickly. Still, I did have time to be astonished. Never, in all my experience, had I seen such color on a Homo sapiens. She'd obviously spent a lot of time in a one-piece bathing suit, because everywhere the sun had touched was freckled. Her cleavage was, but her bosoms weren't, and her belly absolutely glowed. I was so impressed that I said to hell with the Introduction and jumped to Page One. Rose slid under me, but not without many reservations. She felt tense and regretful already.

"Bubber, this is a one time only proposition. I want you to understand that. Are you listening?"

"Repeat?" I said, snuffling in her fanned-out hair.

"I said, this is a —"

"No — repeat? Necessary?"

She smiled and I felt her body relax under me. "You oddball." She put her warning hand on the back of my neck. "You're *so* experienced."

"Repeat?"

"Yes," she said. "Please."

Book II

Book II

Chapter

6

I HAVE HEARD THE EXPERIENCE OF "FALLING IN love" compared to the midair sensation of tripping and falling to the floor on your head.

During the next two months that spring, Rose and I fell in love on our heads. Other lovers have experienced equally blind emotions. The same comatose glances. The strained laughter that ends with heavy breathing. The awkward struggle for balanced positions in back seats, bushes, flower beds — and even once, while night jogging, in a cardboard refrigerator box out behind Banek's Appliance Store. I finished out the school year in a hypnotized state; wedged in the tiny chair-desks of my classrooms, I thought of nothing but Rose's arms and legs and mysterious organs, until all my atoms ached. Hers suffered, too, but she ascribed her pain to guilt. Our age difference seemed too extreme. But it wasn't, really. Though I was younger, I'd already made as many stupid mistakes as any forty-year-old; certainly I was just as handicapped by experience as she. I argued this again and again, with some results.

But probably Rose's body, not my arguments, convinced her that loving me was for the good. The first present I bought her was a blue pair of New Balance running shoes. I'd taken to jogging with Bengal — preparing him for the Great Out-of-Bars — and Rose needed to get in shape, too. The only exercise she'd taken since high school was slap-fighting with her ex-husband, Lonny. So in the evenings, instead of smoking and drinking in her recliner, she came out running with us. Jogging made her feel looser and long-legged at work, she said, and pleasantly exhausted at night.

And running so often, her muscles began to ache and to interest her. With me as her guide, she explored her body quite a bit. By the time I'd graduated we knew her every dent and curve, bone and connecting ligament. It amazed Rose that by exercising, her physical shape was changing. Inch by inch she was becoming someone else. Some evenings after our run, we sat on the kitchen steps under the bug-light and traced each other's muscle groups, while kissing. But at the sound of Randy's Bonneville coasting into position out front, Rose would jump up, slip into her yellow robe, and go sit sloppily in her recliner. By still acting bored and lazy, she kept Shirley from becoming suspicious.

That much hadn't changed. I dated Rose only under the cover of dark, in total secrecy. A concerned mother, she was afraid of the effect her affair with a high school boy would have on her explosive little daughter; on the other hand, *I* was afraid of the effect her daughter would have on that boy. My crippled ear was proof enough that Shirley would disapprove.

So naturally I kept tabs on Shirley through Randy, who told me every detail of every date. He wanted to stay on the good side of his offensive line, and besides, Randy didn't really enjoy kissing without telling. She had told him she'd never been so happy, and she almost meant it. And why not? Randy had wined and dined her all over Houston, even at the high Oiler's Club overlooking the Domed Stadium. Shirley especially liked to sit at that bar near the window, where she could look down on people. This life seemed the one she was meant to live, the life of the moderately wealthy.

But moderate wealth runs out. Randy explained this to her one night while they were drinking Mai Tais on his brother's credit card.

"What do you mean you're broke? Your father owns every clothing store in Waller County."

"I know he does, but he makes me work. All summer, selling string ties."

"Ugh," Shirley said. Somehow she couldn't imagine Handsome Ransom selling string ties. He looked so much more at home in the Oiler's Club.

"So," Randy went on. Shirley's arms were bare but he strained to think clearly. "So we won't be able to come here for your last night."

Randy and Shirley's glances turned longing. They might have actually loved each other, if the issue hadn't been so clouded by sex. Shirley gave up the longing look first, and flounced in her seat.

"Well, what *are* we gonna do? And remember, you promised me that special sex treat. It's a fair trade for the disgusting business you like."

"Ahem!" Randy said, and waited while a wealthily attired waiter cleared their glasses away. Basically he and Shirley traded sex favors; she would do something she found disgusting to him, if he did something he found disgusting to her; they never actually did anything together. Randy leaned across the table and halfway up Shirley's arms.

"Don't worry, *I* always keep my part of these deals," he said. "We'll just have to do it someplace I can afford."

Shirley thought about it on the way home. If she could, she would get out of her part of this latest sex bargain — usually she found a way to do that — but even if she finally gave Ransom what he wanted, it didn't matter. Because the next day her father would pick her up, and then she would never be so happy, for real.

Actually, Rose and I dated only partially in total secrecy. The two best busybodies in town, her neighbors, had guessed. Fat Mr. Finch and his skinny, near-blind wife. Each night that spring they watched their TV out on the porch. One warm evening in late May, as Kojak pursued the bushy-headed degenerate down the tenement fire escape, the Finches heard other footsteps, closer, on the sidewalk out front.

"Who's that?" cranky Mrs. Finch asked her husband. She had cataracts and used his eyes.

"The saucer-eared boy," he said, "jogging with his tiger again. Damnedest country, ain't it? Feebleminded boys get to run up and down the streets with jungle animals. I'm telling you! At least he didn't pilfer no roses tonight."

"Which direction he turn?"

"Toward her house, same as always. And his daddy already passed, in Cznek's truck. I forgot to tell you that."

"You always forget!" his wife scolded. "You *know* how I depend on you." She took away his tub of French onion dip.

As usual Rose was ready for me that night, wearing a Merry Tigers T-shirt and her Irish green running shorts. On the kitchen steps she laced up her New Balance running shoes. They were bright blue and seemed magic to her.

"Where to tonight?" she asked, moving to her elastic pre-running stretches. "And you promised to tell me in a poem."

I cleared my throat, kicked Bengal who was peeing on Shirley's yellow Datsun, and stood straight up. My poem began:

> Mostly we run around in the dark,
> but tonight we're gonna see art.
> Turn right at the dike,
> Wear your diaphragm tight,
> And wiggle when the movie starts.

Rose laughed and took off running without us. We crossed the bahia pasture out back, following cowpaths at an easy pace to the Lifetime Gate at the road. I'd badgered Rose until she'd quit smoking, and her breath came easily as we ran. Bengal's, however, did not. Tigers are not basically long distance animals, and neither are big boys, and by the time we'd reached the bumpy road where the Mexicans lived, there was equal huffing on each end of our leash.

The Mexicans lived on the river's side of the flood dike, and trotting along the top of it we could see the happy bright lights of their hovels. On the other side lay the town, and the huge screen of the Starlight Drive-in. It backed up to the dike, and spreading my letter blanket out on the dense Pangola grass, we felt we were in the presence of a monument. The actors' and actresses' faces were the size of Volkswagens, floating out there above the prairie.

"This is great," Rose said from the Lotus position. "And the bugs aren't even bad. How far did we run?"

"Two miles, maybe three from the look of Bengal." He lay stretched at our feet, exhausted and falling instantly asleep like an animal. "But you shouldn't sprint so hard at the end. He can't keep up."

"Bengal? It's *you*, too, Bigfoot."

Still panting I brushed an ant off the corner of the blanket. "Well, anyway, you shouldn't sprint. It's easy to get injured when you're tired."

"Yes, Coach," she said, "but I'm not tired. Here, you take a rest." She pulled me by the cowlick into her lap, and we sat for a while, cooling down and watching the slow unfolding of the long movie. It was a pleasant, warm, clear night with a Gulf breeze. Through the open car windows below we caught pieces of dialogue, enough to keep track of the plot.

But really the cars were more interesting. Hardly any heads were visible. The whole parking lot seemed engaged in the springtime mating frenzy. Occasionally a boy would run back to the men's room, where he'd emerge in a moment tearing a prophylactic package open with his teeth. The orgy below must have set Rose thinking about her daughter, because she asked:

"Bubber, what sort of girl *is* she? I'm worried."

I didn't answer for a moment. Rose loved her scary little daughter and I didn't want to hurt her with the truth. Besides, I didn't know the truth. Shirley was sneaky, stubborn, and manipulative now, but she could grow up into something else entirely.

"Don't worry. She'll probably turn out a mysterious woman, like you."

Rose laughed. She knew the truth better than I. "Mysterious women aren't made from strange girls. And Shirley's definitely strange."

"That's a fine attitude for a mother to have."

Rose laughed again, this time at me. She thought I was cutely old-fashioned. I didn't mind — Rose had a good laugh — and with my head in her lap I could hear the sound it made internally.

Rose noticed where I was concentrating, and reached down to shake my head by my nose. "*Why* do you take such an interest in my anatomy?"

"Dark reasons, I suppose."

"No, really, why?"

I hadn't thought about it but I answered promptly. "Because you're different from me. I mean, you're a different build of person."

"I'd better be," she said, "or we're having even stranger sex than I thought."

"You mean we're having strange sex?"

"No," she said tentatively, then ran a hand through my hair. "Just different."

I hoped she also meant better. I knew this much: I'd never have better sex if I lived to Dad's age, and I didn't need much experience to know that. I rose up to kiss a favorite freckle on the side of her nose, then sank down to enjoy the movie.

But that was difficult. It was *King Kong*, the new one, and the only good part was the amazing giant gorilla machine. It lifted the screaming, scantily clad woman so gently that it could almost have been animal, and the eyes behind the gorilla mask seemed strangely intelligent, like Bengal's. The poor fellow, Bengal, knew something was going on in his life, something was in store for him in the Great Out-of-Bars, but he couldn't fathom what. I reached down to massage his neck, but he was making noises through his lips, having a tiger-dream.

"Don't wake him," Rose whispered, peeling off her T-shirt. "You can massage me."

This caused me to sit up vigorously and shed my shirt and shorts. Occasionally Rose fell into sudden moods and I'd learned to take advantage. Tonight it might have been the mating frenzy below, the mention of strange sex, or the monumental, nearly naked woman on the horizon. Anyway, I helped her out of her brassiere as I gave her ear a preliminary sniff.

"I guess Man invented foundation garments for women like you. Otherwise, you'd bust your jaw the first mile."

"Bubber!" Rose said. She liked to say "Bubber!" and act shocked. "Take your nose out of my ear."

"But you redheads really stink. I mean, it's a special smell."

She laughed, lay down, and I began to massage. But I

wasn't in much of a mood for it tonight. I'd begun to want to know more about Rose than her muscles. In a way, she'd limited our relationship to that. And I wanted to see farther into our future than Bengal could see into his. I worked on her fuzzy legs and asked:

"What was your father like?"

Rose sat up on her elbows. "That's a strange question out of the blue." But she thought about it. Her father had been dead twelve years now. "He was a lot of things, but mostly grumpy in the mornings. He hated to get up and feed the horses. We had about a hundred of them, counting foals." She was smiling, remembering her old man. She hadn't thought about him enough lately.

"And what did you like most about him?" I asked.

"Oh, that's easy: the way he always complimented me. Even when he was shouting about me leaving the pasture gate open, he'd stop and say I had a nice way of carrying my head. He was the national goat-roping champion one year."

"He sounds a little like Dad — he frequently compares me with livestock. But really, you'd like my dad — why don't you let me introduce you?"

Rose laughed a little cruelly. "You'd have to goat-rope and drag me back there. I lied about it that night, but those snakes made me wet my pants."

"Now, now," I said. "They're not so bad. Several of them have personalities."

"I'm sure," Rose said. "But I'm *not* going."

We grew quiet a moment. The issue of her meeting Dad had become an issue.

"Sometimes," I said, moving to her hips. "Sometimes I

wish you'd let me talk about our future. When Shirley leaves tomorrow, you'll be all alone. Wouldn't it be better if I moved in?"

Rose had no comment. She watched the big screen, where a sedated King Kong was bound by chains in the hold of a ship. I scooted up, my chest to her bare back.

"Heck, I don't keep loving you a secret. You're the one who's so worried about reputations."

She had to pay attention to me; I was speaking directly into her ear.

"I've waited a long time to be all alone, Bubber. And besides, what would your old-fashioned father say?"

"Charlie knows who I'm seeing. He says it's hormonal — but he can't squawk, the way he's chasing after Claudine. A Classic Second Adolescence."

"Well, it probably *is* hormonal."

"What difference does that make? Just admit you love me and forget the reasons. You're a piss-poor excuse for a romantic."

Sighing, she rolled over to face me, and tried to decide how to get me off her back. It wasn't that I was a burden; it was just that I was too young. She'd already passed certain points in her life — getting married, having children, finding a career. Where would a nineteen-year-old, big-eared boy fit in?

But it was a nice warm night, and she decided not to brutalize me with her doubts. "Look, Bubber. We're both having fun, but I don't want you so wrapped up in this. In a few days you start your summer job, and in two months you'll be off to college. I want you thinking about *your* future, not ours."

"Sure," I said, though her words had hardly registered. When Rose rolled over like that, her bosoms glided off to the sides, and I always became entranced when they moved.

Rose saw where I was looking, and reached up to touch my hair. "Your cowlick," she said, "makes your head look like a partially open can."

I raised my eyes to hers. She was looking at me with the simplest goodwill. She appreciated me, my looks, my humor; and I felt at the peak of my life. Gradually we began gazing at each other in the way aching lovers do. Our passion was painful and spontaneous, the way it had been the night we screwed in the refrigerator box.

But this night's pain was different. It was real. I discovered this after I'd slipped over on Rose. She began wiggling in a very unusual manner.

"Something wrong?" I snuffled in her ear.

"Isn't something biting you?"

"Yes," I said. "Now that you mention it."

She slapped her thigh and brought the something up to look at. It was a fire ant, with friends. Apparently we'd spread the blanket over their home, disgruntling them.

"Ouch!" I said.

"Ooy!" Rose replied.

We jumped up and began slapping ourselves and each other. The sudden noise spooked Bengal, who woke with a start. Strange little things were attacking his legs. He roared; I shouted; Rose cursed; Bengal decided to flee. I chased along the dike after his leash, running slow with a large erection, while Rose hollered after us. Then giving up, she gathered our things and ran, too, with one arm holding down her large bosoms.

We must have made quite a spectacle, naked on top of the dike, because later that night I got an angry phone call from Randy. I answered expecting the usual play-by-play, but he was mad.

"Jesus H. Christ, you stupid numbskull! You nearly ruined my last night of sex. Luckily I got mine before she saw you."

A chill swept through me. I sat down on Dad's reading chair and scratched at my ant bites.

"You were there, at the Starlight?"

"We were."

"Shirley saw?"

"She saw."

A larger chill swept me. "What did she do? We didn't hear any shouts."

"Oh," Randy said, getting sarcastic. "She didn't even open her mouth. She did something worse. I don't know what she has against her mother, but she got so mad she didn't even collect her sex favor, thank God."

"Something worse? You said she did something worse?"

Randy paused. "She started thinking."

"Oh, God."

"That's right, start praying when Shirley starts thinking. It's lucky for me she's leaving tomorrow, or I might not have an offensive guard."

I sat a few minutes with the phone in my hand before I realized Randy had hung up. I hung up, too, and looked blankly around. From their rows of snakequariums about fifty snakes watched me. The room was still, except for the swishing of the ceiling fan, and the sound of an approaching pickup dragging a mailbox.

After Sinclair slid to a stop, the four occupants had a hard time getting out. At Claudine's insistence Dad had brought Loops to her beer joint, and on the drive home he'd lassoed the four old friends. When they got more or less untangled they filed inside, each shouldering a piece of the fat snake.

"I told you," Claudine was saying. "Snake Night was a big success. Billy said business was up forty percent."

Dad grinned, laying his part of Loops on the linoleum. "I knew snakes would get popular again."

Sinclair might have debated him, but Loops had hooked his tail around the old fellow's neck. "Gaggh!" he said and fell down. "Wugh! Ahght!"

They all rushed back to unfasten Loops's tail. Still gagging, Sinclair got up and struck Dad, then let his sister and girlfriend help him over to Dad's chair. That's when they noticed me, still in my daze.

"Here's Bubber!" Lucy Taylor hollered. She was getting deaf. "Without no shirt!"

"And *look* at him," Claudine added. "He's the picture of Samson in my Bible."

I smiled hello and flexed a weary biceps. "Able to stop a locomotive by showing my armpit. Here, Sinclair, you take the chair."

He waved me away and stomped down the hall for a Pearl beer, while old Dad glared at me. Men shouldn't be seen shirtless by ladies. "Don't encourage the boy, Claudine," he said. "He's got an illicit mistress and no more morals than a Brahman bull."

"Dad, I'm in no mood to argue morals tonight, and I wish you'd quit saying 'Durn.' Claudine, can't you at least get him to say 'damn'?"

She smiled. "I'm working on it, but he's a pretty hopeless case."

"Humpf," Dad said, sitting on his desk beside her. Claudine wore a white western shirt, a denim skirt, aluminum-colored hair, and a section of her favorite snake, Loops. Over her shoulder, the big snake dropped his ropey tongue out and looked blindly around. The night out at a beer joint had plainly exhausted him. Dad petted him affectionately where his ears should be.

Gradually Loops slid onto Dad's shoulders, too, and was lacing him and Claudine together. Dad gave Claudine a simple, fond look. Claudine returned it. Maybe the two of them being crushed by Loops reminded her of another picture in her Bible.

Later I'd pulled a chair up to my bedroom window and was brooding in the dark over a glass of buttermilk. The lights of town twinkled off across the prairie; the rice dryer's red light blinked. So, Shirley had seen us, and she had started thinking. If she used only ten percent of her mind, she could come up with some awful punishments. Good fortune was on our side, though, since Shirley was leaving tomorrow.

Below my window the four old friends walked out to Sinclair's truck. Dad reached into the truckbed and took out a small canvas Braniff bag. Then he and Claudine tiptoed back inside. As they passed under my window I heard Dad whisper, "His lights are out; he must have fallen asleep." He said it like a sneaky teenager, sneaking his girlfriend into the house.

This made me suspicious enough to creep to the stairwell, where from the darkness I could see them tiptoeing into the kitchen. Claudine set about mixing two glasses of chocolate milk, while Dad watched on nervously. He kept putting his hands in his pockets, then taking them out.

"Maybe we ought not . . . ," he whispered. "And I shouldn't. . . . I'll just drive you home."

"You can't drive at night, you know that." Claudine took the milk past him to his bedroom, where she lay her nightgown out on the bed and brushed her hair at the vanity. I could hear Dad swallowing hard at his door — a sound resembling a drain coming unclogged. A woman was brushing her hair in his bedroom! Still, he seemed unable to move his feet.

"Come on in, Charlie," she said. "It's as natural as rain."

"All right," he whispered, his old heart leaping. "In a minute." He stood a little longer, watching her brush and savoring the moment. Then he tiptoed to the icebox and took something out. Before he closed the bedroom door I heard him say, "Chilled bran muffins. Try one with the milk. They're real good, and they make tomorrow easy."

Chapter

7

BUT FOR ME TOMORROW WOULDN'T BE SO EASY. I prepared for it with a sweaty night dreaming. I don't recall every nightmare, but they included driving-twisting-road dreams, diving-from-great-height dreams, and swimming-among-many-alligators. The last one before waking was a closet dream. I walked down a long hall of closets opening each one, and each one contained little Shirley. She was armed with a bar of Ivory soap in a sock, which she hit me with. Thanking her, I closed each door and moved on. Whatever the dark implications of this dream, they gave me an iron-spike headache, and I awoke bewildered, bound hand and foot in my knotted sheets, wondering who I was, where I was, and what sort of life I'd led. But gradually more important questions came to mind. Had Shirley killed her mother early last night, or had she waited until Rose was asleep? I untied myself from the bed and threw on my clothes.

Downstairs, Dad was awake, too — a rare occurrence. He slipped out of his bedroom, closing the door so quickly that he caught his robe, which he tried to brush off as a normal accident.

"Hm? Oh, yeah. Ah! Bubber! Good to see you, son. Up bright and early. Going somewhere?"

I was wolfing down a breakfast of bananas and aspirin. "Rose's house. I'm trying to prevent a murder."

"Hm? Oh, yeah. Good idea," Dad said, distracted. His mood was happily guilty, but he wanted to have a man-to-man. Following me out to the car he tied and retied his robe sash a dozen times. I got in and started up.

"Dad, look, if you've got something to tell me, talk fast."

He leaned leisurely at my window. "Me? Oh, hell, I got nothing to say."

"Well then, let me go. Really I'm —"

"But now that you mention it," he interrupted. "Maybe there is something." He stretched his neck and looked down. "Ah, why don't you and me quit arguing over morals for a while. Something's come up and I need to forget mine."

Looking down, Dad seemed to be watching me. I guess he needed my permission to romp. I gave his old hand a friendly swat, one senseless lover to another.

I knocked on my mistress's screen door, fearful her daughter would answer, but Rose came, sleep tossled and fragrant from a night under the covers. Since she wasn't dead or heavily bandaged, I assumed she'd slept in total ignorance. "Where's Shirley?" was my first question.

"Bubber! Go away!" Rose answered, glancing over her shoulder.

I thought I'd better come in. "Aw, open the door. You never told me you stunk so much in the morning."

"Shh. Shirley's up!"

"I figured she would be. What time's her callous brute father getting here?"

I opened the door myself and Rose stepped back out of kissing range. She didn't know why I was here or what I'd do, or how violently Shirley would react. From the kitchen we heard a spoon hit the cereal bowl, followed by a small angry grunt. Then little Shirley appeared. She wore a blue Peter Pan blouse, and she looked young, almost innocent, and icily composed. Rose made up a reason for my presence.

"Oh, honey, Bubber just came to tell you goodbye. Isn't that nice?"

Shirley smirked at the lie and looked from her mother to me. "Don't let me intrude. Go ahead, Momma, french-kiss my ex-boyfriend."

Rose stared at her daughter.

"She and Randy saw," I explained, "everything."

Rose looked immediately worried. Shirley knew? Why wasn't she shouting or throwing things? Confused, Rose ran a hand through her hair and decided to retreat.

"I have to get dressed for work, Shirley," she said, walking off, "maybe you'd like to yell at me in my room?"

Shirley smirked after her mother, then at me. She picked up her pig bristle hairbrush from the counter and strolled into the parlor, touching furniture and stroking her long hair. We hadn't been alone together in some time and the atmosphere was thick. I followed a few steps behind, just out of striking range.

"You're smoldering," I said. "I can see that. But we were just exercising. Jogging."

"*Naked?*" She turned quickly, which made me flinch, and looked me slowly over. "You really *are* the most perverted boy I ever dated. But," she said, growing dangerously thoughtful, "I'm glad all this finally happened." She looked out the front window. "And for your information, Daddy is *not* a brute. He said he'd leave at the crack of dawn, when I told him about this den of iniquity."

"Shirley, please. It's all my fault. Your mother was helpless in my clutches. You'll feel better if you lose control and clobber me. In the groin," I added, "if you want."

"Clobber your own groin," she snapped, "but do it quietly. I'm listening for Daddy's car."

Rose returned, hastily dressed in her whites and still strapping on her wristwatch. I guess she feared bloodshed if she were gone too long. And she wanted to talk to me alone.

"Honey, you better go straighten your room. I don't want you leaving it a mess."

Shirley gave her mother a controlled, superior look. "*You* don't have the right to give me orders anymore. But I'm going, because *I've* got something to do. You just sit down with your high school boyfriend." With the utmost sassy control she glided away down the hall. Her self-control, however, disintegrated in her room. We could hear her growling as she tore posters down from the walls and jerked drawers onto the floor. Rose got a cup of coffee, turned on the *Today Show*, and dropped herself into the pocket of the La-Z-Boy.

"How?"

"On the dike, when the ants attacked us."

Rose gave me a hard look, sat up in her chair, then sank back even further. *Why* had she ever gotten involved with me? It was fun, sure, but was it worth the wreckage? Down the hall came the wood-splintering crash of a bureau hitting the floor. Rose listened. Strangely, she seemed accustomed to the angry sounds of a daughter in the house. And stranger, she'd probably miss them. I tried to help out with these feelings.

"By August, she'll be ready to come home, from what you've told me about Lonny."

"That's a thought," Rose said, sarcastically. "That's a nice thought. At least her father is a worse influence than me."

Back in high school Rose had been one of those headstrong sixteen-year-olds who rebel against authority by dating servicemen. When she was two weeks overdue, Spec. 1 Butts stopped calling. Luckily or unluckily, Rose's older brother was an old-fashioned boy with a heart the size of a garbage can. He called Lonny up at the airbase and invited him out deep-sea fishing. Stupid Lonny accepted. Out of sight of land, Ben pushed Lonny overboard. Then he drove in circles around him until Lonny thought he'd never see Galveston again. "The poor guy," Rose said when she'd told me the story, "he was as green as me at the wedding. We spent the honeymoon throwing up."

Later, Ben regretted everything. Having Lonny for a brother-in-law had cost him ten or twelve thousand dollars and several hundred late-night phone calls. He moved to California — or as Rose put it, "out of lending distance from Lonny."

Remembering this, I sat down on the arm of her chair. "Maybe young girls need to clean their systems of Lonnies. She'll be better off, wait and see."

Rose looked up. "Thanks," she said, and took my hand. I had caused her trouble, but somehow I could still be comforting.

Down the hall the noise had subsided. Shirley had broken every stick of furniture she could, and she felt somewhat relieved. Still, there was something else she had to do; clearly she had thought about doing it all night.

She crossed the hall to the bathroom, where she closed and bolted the door. She stayed inside a very long time, and came out relaxed and smiling. It was an unscrupulous little smile that didn't even flicker when she saw me sitting with her mother. Suspicious behavior, I thought, followed by more. She came right over and plumped down on Rose's other arm, very comfortable, as though we were an ordinary family in front of the TV. Rose got worried again.

"What took you so long in the bathroom?"

"It's morning, after breakfast — what do people normally do then? Jeez, Momma, you're really gonna miss me. There won't be anyone here to check up on." She repeated her dishonest little smile, then looked at me. "Or maybe there will be."

On TV, Tom Brokaw was interviewing a thick-tongued

Norwegian psychiatrist about mood swings and murder/suicides, and Shirley feigned interest in that. But she couldn't feign too long; depressing subjects irritated her. She had more control over her life than that. She brushed her hair for a while, then said:

"Oh, Momma, I want you to know I left a surprise for you. When you get it, think about me — and about all those lectures you gave about the right way to behave. You, too, Bubber. You may be involved."

After ten o'clock it got too hot to sit inside, and we all moved out to the porch. Neither Rose nor I had figured out the riddle of Shirley's surprise; I guess the heat had made us stupid. Shirley herself seemed to have forgotten it. She made me drag her footlocker out to the pecan tree, while she stared down the ranch road from the porch steps. This was the day she'd waited for ever since the divorce, and she was concentrating so hard she could have transported Lonny down the highway on her brainwaves.

At noon Rose called Mrs. White to trade today's day duty for night, and she came back out with a tray of tuna fish sandwiches. Shirley took one look at them. "Ugh! They'll spoil my breath. Daddy hates the smell of fish — you know that." Naturally, I asked if I could eat hers, and she smiled again. "You'll need all your strength."

Finally, around three, Lonny Butts showed up. Shirley saw his El Camino first and raced down to the pecan to meet him. Rose stepped outside from doing the ironing, smelling of lovely steam and spray starch, and stood in front of me with her arms folded.

It appeared that Lonny had brought along his latest

floozy — to show her off, I guess. She was a woman who liked to be seen. Her hairdo stood two feet taller than her head and was the color of the El Camino chrome. She nearly sat in Lonny's lap, but he nudged her off, got out, and put on his auctioneer's Stetson before he kissed Shirley lightly on the forehead. Shirley took the kiss like the blow of an ax, staring at the floozy climbing out behind.

"Sorry I'm late, sugar. La Vonne couldn't get me out of bed this morning, no matter what she tried." He winked back at the woman.

"La Vonne?"

"Yeah, sugar," La Vonne said standing up. She was very tall, very manicured and coiffed, and she wore a low-cut red jumpsuit. Basically she was the kind of woman they make blow-up sex dolls after. When she pranced up to Shirley, her big bosoms juggled. "She's so *small*," she said of Shirley, petting her hair with several long fingernails.

Shirley winced. Lonny didn't notice. He hugged them both.

"You two are gonna get on fine. We got a spare bedroom in the condo, and La Vonne has already bought you a new air mattress."

"You're married?"

"Hell no, not until La Vonne quits her job at Figure World. I won't have a wife working — you know that — but what the hell, it pays the bills." He hugged them both again, up to his neck in women who loved him.

"Lonny," Rose said from the porch. "I'd like to speak to you about bills, too, if you can untangle yourself."

Lonny grinned up, and spoke sideways to La Vonne. "That's the hairy-legged ex. I told you she was sarcastic."

La Vonne smiled in a frozen manner.

"Sugar," Lonny told his daughter, "throw that trunk in the truck for me, will you? You remember my bad back."

"I'd help," La Vonne said, following her man to the porch steps, "but I might chip a nail."

Lonny ambled ahead of her shaking out a cigarette. I hated the smooth way he did it. He was a good-looking man, I'd admit that, but I'm glad to say he chain-smoked and his lungs probably resembled briquettes. He struck a match on the sole of his loud lizard boots. He was a smaller man than I imagined, but his hair and sideburns were longer.

" 'Lo, Rose."

"About the bills," she began, setting her feet. "You're ten months late on child support. You know that money goes into Shirley's college account."

Lonny ignored her, sucking in smoke and smirking at me. "You the boy? I heard you been romping nude with my wife."

"*Ex*-wife," Rose said. "And that's not the subject."

"No, it's the right subject," I said, stepping around her. "I'd like to discuss it." I didn't need to flex my arms; they were already very ready.

Rose touched my shoulder from behind and said lightly, "Quit playing the he-man and go help Shirley. She looks like she's getting a hernia."

I departed huffily, breathing tuna fish on Lonny as I passed. Once the truck was loaded Shirley and I leaned against it listening to the adults act like children. I don't know why, but I still liked little Shirley. Maybe it was her predicament. She'd expected to spend time with her father this summer, and now she'd be sharing him with La Vonne. La Vonne wasn't the sort of woman who shared well.

"So *you're* the ex," she was saying, hands on hips and scanning Rose's figure. She obviously thought she alone resided on the upper limbs of woman's evolution. "Lonny's told me *so* much about you."

"Funny," Rose said, returning the scan. "He's said nothing at all about you. The other one he talked about a lot."

La Vonne didn't have to think; she was experienced at eating smaller fish. "Yes, he had the same low opinion of the both of you." She hooked her arm into his. Rose gave her a sincere look.

"La Vonne, any woman Lonny thinks highly of has got all my sympathy. Now about the bills — Shirley can't go to college if you don't work."

"He's working," La Vonne said, "but you don't know how the cattle business is." Her tone implied Rose had no sympathy, which she didn't where her daughter's well-being was concerned. The discussion continued under arctic conditions.

Beside me, Shirley snorted.

"Don't worry," I told her. "In a week you'll have *her* sleeping on the air mattress."

"Harumpf!" Shirley spat. "In a week there won't be anything left of La Vonne but some hair in the sink."

I don't think Shirley meant she'd ax-murder La Vonne, but there was a determined look in her little blue eyes.

Before they all left, Rose came down to hug Shirley goodbye, and Shirley actually hugged her back. Then Lonny told his daughter to sit by the window, because La Vonne didn't like the wind tilting her hairdo, and La Vonne practically scooted into his lap.

We watched them go, then Rose went to the steps and sat down, depressed. I stood awkwardly beside her, thinking of cheerful things to say.

"Cute family. Before the summer's over they'll be biting each other."

Rose looked up, shading her eyes from the afternoon sun. "Not now, Bubber, please. I think I'd like to be alone."

Then she got to her feet and went inside to clean Shirley's room. There, she sat on the bed amid the wreckage for a long while, slowly pulling poster tacks out of the wall. And when it was finally time to go to work, she got up and gratefully went. She never even saw me, peeping in the window.

It wasn't difficult to figure out Rose's problem: an empty house. I'd gone through the same experience myself, after Mom died. For months I thought I heard her in the kitchen, lifting the heavy iron skillet with a grunt, and I sorely missed the exuberant sound of her blowing her nose. A quiet, empty house; a distinct isolation; I knew it well.

So, I moved in. I thought about doing it gradually — first a toothbrush, then a few T-shirts, and finally a jockstrap hanging on the shower knob — but by nature I'm a sudden disaster.

Rose came home the next morning, dog tired from working all night, to find me painting the porch. My cardboard suitcase stood on the unpainted path to the screen door. Rose saw it, veered to the porch steps, and sat down, pulling her nurse's cap off. I believe she also groaned.

"There's no use resisting," I said, painting the steps below her. "Think of me as a Force of Nature. A tidal wave or something."

She sighed, cap in hands, and looked out to the prairie. The rising sun had begun to burn the dew off the young rice heads. "I didn't expect my life to go like this."

"Aw, it's not so bad. Move up a step or two, will you? Do you like the color? I call it freckle brown."

Rose started to smile but failed when Bengal roared out back.

"Him, too?"

I nodded. "After Dad quit kicking the furniture, he said if I was going to disgrace the family, he wouldn't feed my tiger. And anyway, it's time he got out from behind bars."

Rose got up wearily and walked the path to the door. She stopped to look at my suitcase. "Bubber, can I possibly get rid of you?"

"No ma'am." I crawled behind her, painting the path closed. "I'm stuck on you like a tick."

Her expression softened; she shook the cap crimps out of her hair, then sighed again. "All right, but you're sleeping in Shirley's room. The rent's seventy-five a month and we'll work the board out."

"Shirley's room?" I said, but she'd taken my suitcase

inside. By the time I'd finished painting the path she had put clean sheets on the bed and opened my suitcase.

"Hey, what do you think you're doing? I'm not sleeping here."

Rose straightened up and put a stack of T-shirts in a broken drawer. "Like it or leave it. The other bedroom's mine, Bubber."

She spoke in a no-nonsense tone, and scratching my cowlick I followed her down the hall to her room. It was an ordinary room by some standards, with yellow drapes and green walls, but it had one remarkable feature. A queen-sized waterbed. I stared at it longingly from the door. Rose started to get undressed, turning away.

"You go on. I'm tired and this is my room."

"No it's not," I grumbled. "It's *our* room, but you just won't let me sleep here."

Rose smiled over her shoulder. She'd unbuttoned the front of her dress but didn't want to go any further for fear of stimulating me.

"I don't understand," I said. "I don't understand why. The other night you said you'd never —"

"The other night I learned a lesson," she said, getting firm again. "I'm just *not* the type to run around with high school boys. Now if you have to stay here, you'll live your own life. You'll go out on your own dates, just like me. And you'll sleep in the other room."

"Like heck I will. That room's for the kids. I might be nineteen, but you love me and I'm your man. And I'm gonna sleep on the sofa — where the ejected man's sup-*pos*ed to sleep."

"Suit yourself," she hollered after me, "but Shirley's bed's more comfortable."

I rumbled down the hall to the parlor, convinced that the sofa was the right wrong place to sleep. I tossed myself on it angrily, and the whole frame shook. Then important pieces of the sofa splintered, and it collapsed at one end. I guess my angry toss was too heavy. I got up to look after the damage. Two legs snapped off at the ankles, and one support strut shattered.

Rose came padding barefoot down the hall. Was she coming to apologize and throw herself on me? Hardly. She wore her green running shorts and carried her New Balance shoes.

"Breaking furniture?" she asked, going to the record player. "Do you want to pay for these things by the week, or in one lump sum?"

I looked at the lopsided sofa, the two broken legs in my hands. The whole thing sloped violently to one end.

"It's more healthful to sleep with your head lower than your feet," I explained.

"I know," Rose said, smiling cruelly. "In my waterbed, I do."

She seemed intent on running me off with meanness, but a boy who lives with a tiger is used to that. I set about mending her sofa while she selected some old Beatles albums. To "Hard Day's Night" she did her pre-running stretches. I watched as I tried to fix the sofa with Elmer's Glue. But Rose looked so lovely doing her toe-crosses that I nearly glued my hand to the sofa's stump legs. Finally I just stuck the feet on any which-a-way. There had to be some way to get into her waterbed. After all, we did still love each other. As she got down to do her situps, she caught me watching her.

"Whenever you look at me sideways like that, I get nervous. Hold my feet and tell me what you're plotting."

I scooted over and wiped the glue off my fingers. "How long have we been dating?"

She thought, grunting with each situp. "Two months, nearly three. Why?"

"Well, I was just thinking: for every step I've made with you, I've had to get something broken."

"That sounds terrible. And it's not true."

"Sure it is. You forgot to drop by, and Bengal broke my skin. And then there was the Round-up dance."

Rose was silent, surveying my crooked ear. I could have included the Oriental Night bombardment and subsequent headache, too.

"What's your point?" she asked, suspiciously.

"Me? Oh, I'm using guilt to get into your bed—I admit that. And since I've got to break something, I'm trying to decide. Do you have a least favorite leg?"

Rose fell back from her situps and looked at me. I tried to look cute, like a bed toy. Probably it was my funny expression that made hers soften. She sat up and played with my cowlick.

"You don't have to break anything else. The sofa's enough."

I couldn't believe my ear. Had I won? Was this victory?

"You mean it's okay? We're illicit lovers again?"

Rose smiled at the enthusiasm in my voice. "For the

summer. For the summer *only*. And I don't want the town to know."

"Of course not! I'll throw leaves on my car every night. Absolutely. Come on —" I jumped up and pulled Rose to her feet. "Let's dance!" The Beatles were singing "Till There Was You."

But Rose put her palm to my chest. "You can't. I forgot to tell you something when I came out."

"What?"

She smiled. "It's morning, you dope. And you have to go to work."

Chapter

8

SEVERAL THINGS OF INTEREST HAPPENED THAT summer, none of which had to do with my job. I worked on the road crew for Texas Tarmacadam, laying reinforcing rods in the blistering sun. It was the low, dirty, heavy sort of work normally given to high school graduates. All morning long the big prairie sun baked our brains in our hardhats as we dragged the steel rods off of the flatbed. Then our supervisor, a tobacco-chewing pug-ugly who'd lost his job with the prison system, swore and spat at us until we got the rods laid out in a grid. That was the easy part, before the afternoon heat rose up and the deafening concrete machine started spewing goo. Diesel smoke and cancer-causing mists blew across us as we wired the rod grid together. To do this we walked stooped over in the shape of a question mark; it was like tying your shoes in Hell all afternoon, for under two dollars an hour.

But when the evening whistle blew, no one was luckier than me. My friends climbed in their cars and went home to parents who misunderstood them, and I drove home to Rose. She worked from seven to four, so she usually had supper ready for us. That was the one drawback to living with Rose — her suppers. She couldn't cook at all, but she tried. I kidded her constantly and suggested countless times that we just eat my usual, but she wouldn't hear of eating chicken pot pies. Her recipes had been passed down from her mother, another dangerous cook.

After the sun sank (so we wouldn't be seen together) the three of us would go running the ranch roads. For Rose it had become an addiction, and for Bengal it was a nightly feast. He'd gotten used to living out-of-bars now, on his chain in the backyard, and whenever we jogged up to a road-kill, he pounced on it so naturally that he might have killed it himself. All day long on his chain he listened intently for the wild call of automobile brakes, and drooled over the smell of burnt rubber.

"I wish he wouldn't chew that armadillo so loud," I panted one night. "It makes my leg wound tingle." Rose was running in place beside me.

"Ha!" she said, "he probably took lessons in lip smacking from you. I couldn't even hear the music tonight."

"Well," I kidded, "your supper was so good I forgot myself. Chipped beef on macaroni — and who else could have thought to add frozen peas."

"Damn you!" Rose snatched off my ballcap and ran ahead. "Catch up if you can, Bigfoot. I can't wait. I've got a race to run next month."

The race she spoke of was the Houston 10,000, through Memorial Park. I dreaded it, but Rose wanted to see if she could accomplish the thing, and I thought she could. I didn't mention this earlier, but in the beginning Rose had carried a few extra pounds. Not that that mattered, of course, but now her fuzzy legs were well toned. At night I craved the sound of her taking a shower. Because after a shower she usually put in her diaphragm.

One night I lay listening to the running water, floating on our waterbed. Sleeping on it was like sleeping on a lily pad. The bedside radio was playing, an opera. Rose liked them but to me they sounded like family squabbles in Italian. I was rolling over to turn it off when Rose came in, wrapped in a large blue towel.

"Don't," she said. "This is the good part — where Ferucio drives a dagger in his heart."

She sat on the bed wiping the wet hair back from her ear. Ferucio continued to holler in great pain. After a while I began to get impatient. Rose was nearly naked on the lily pad, and Ferucio was taking his sweet time dying. He must have stumbled around the stage squalling for fifteen minutes.

Finally Rose sighed, clicked the radio off, and smiled down at me. All had gone well for Ferucio — his lover had slain herself, too — and now I hoped Rose would make the waiting worthwhile. Instead she lay out on the bed still wrapped in the blue towel. Tragic opera put her in a thoughtful mood.

"I got another letter from Shirley today."

"You did? What's the news from the front?"

Rose smiled. Shirley's letters always contained tidbits of gossip about Lonny and La Vonne. Shirley had been unable to run La Vonne up a tree — in fact, La Vonne had run Shirley up one. She'd complained incessantly in bed about having Shirley underfoot all day, so Lonny had forced Shirley to take a job. Actually La Vonne found it for her, in front of the Rexall where she'd got her start. "It's a Fotomat," Shirley had written, "and if it was a little longer I could take two steps. That bitch! She wears wigs, too — did you know that? And you wouldn't believe how she takes advantage of Daddy, now that he's lost his job. His closet is full to the neckties — with *her* wigheads. It's disgusting to see a grown man dig through wigheads to find his boots!"

"Oh," Rose said, still thinking about her daughter's letter, "she threatens to expose us to the community again."

I sat up. "That does it! I'd better go get the knives. We'll need to slay ourselves." Rose laughed, and I asked seriously, "You're not having your doubts again?"

Rose shook her head, smiling as though she had many doubts. Then she thought about it and petted my hand (which lay on her toweled bosom).

"No, not really. But life will be *much* simpler when you're gone. For one thing I'll be able to jog in the daylight."

She reached to turn out the reading light, but I stopped her. I wanted to see her reaction when I said:

"Rose, honey, look: let's get this thing out in the open."

"You mean, make a public display of our wanton immorality?"

"Don't kid, I'm serious. I'm tired of throwing leaves on my car. And before you say no, just listen: We'll show ourselves at the Fourth of July parade. I have to take Bengal in his circus trailer anyway."

"Well —" Rose said. She didn't like to be left out of plans that involved Bengal.

"Well nothing." I snapped out the light. "We might just as well be seen, everybody's heard from the Finches anyway. And I'll ask Dad and Claudine to come. It's a perfect time to introduce you."

I thought about it some more, and it seemed a marvelous idea. But from Rose's silence she seemed unconvinced. "Don't worry," I said. "Just talk to Dad about horses; he'll love you. And we'll use Sinclair's truck and trailer hitch. Don't worry about a thing."

"Bubber," Rose said slowly, "why is it that every time you tell me not to worry, I start."

"A lack of faith, a total lack of faith. But don't worry, it'll all be solved by exposing yourself. Starting now."

"Now?" Rose said in the dark.

"*Right* now." I began to rub her trapezius. "And let's begin by taking off that towel."

Sinclair said no one could drive his truck but him and unfortunately we relented. While he and I hitched up the trailer, Dad and Rose chatted. They seemed at ease together and when I came up, wiping hitch grease off on my jeans, they were laughing about nothing very funny. Which I took to be a good sign.

"I didn't know your daddy was Jim O'Leary," Dad said. "He wasn't a deadbeat like most horsemen. Always real prompt with my bills. But remember that time he took delivery of them Davenport Arabians — he and the Colonel ran off to get drunk — left you, me, and some big-footed fellow —"

"My brother," Rose said. "Ben. The three of us did all the worming ourselves."

"Why I'm surprised you remember. You couldn't of been but six."

"Oh, I remember because I got my wrist dislocated that day, and you found some Adolph's meat tenderizer in your truck."

"Good for man and beast," Dad said. "I bet the swelling went down."

"It did. And you charged Dad for it, too."

Dad laughed. "Always real prompt with his bills."

On the drive to the staging area in town, Dad sat up front to share the wheel with Sinclair, while Claudine, Lucy Taylor, Rose, and I rode on lawnchairs in the truckbed. Rose wore blue and as we drove into town the breeze lifted her shoulder-length hair. My, her hair looked red in the sun. I reached over and asked if she was comfortable. She gave me a tight smile.

"I will be in an hour, when it's over."

"Rose is a little nervous," I explained to the others. "She's never made a public spectacle of herself."

Claudine laughed. "Bubber, you're gonna drive us all to drink."

"Any excuse," said Lucy Taylor, already tipsy in her chair from a can of Pearl. Dad and Sinclair were also drinking cans up front, wrestling over the steering wheel. I began to feel uncomfortable myself; Rose and I shared a miserable glance.

That afternoon was hot and sunny, and the spectators, who lined the curbs awaiting the parade, wore hats or held newspapers over their heads. From the staging area behind the old depot we could hear the noisy Jaycee band and the dense murmurings of the waiting crowds. The staging area was hopping, too, with Texas Rangerettes practicing their high baton tosses, among den mothers chasing packs of excited, disobedient Cub Scouts. Our high school marching band, the Merry Tigers, were unpacking their instruments, and the Waller County Mounted Posse was trying to agitate a small herd of antique Texas longhorns. The cattle were bunched together, asleep on their feet.

Deputy Dozel saw our truck and ran over with a worried look. "Them cows are unconscious, Charlie. Come over and give Mismole a hand."

Doc Mismole was the new young vet fresh from Texas A&M, and no one thought much of him yet. He was sitting in his vet van with his head in his hands. The whooping posse couldn't get the longhorns to budge. They just stood on the street corner and blinked, like a herd of satisfied dope addicts.

Dad climbed out of the truck and spat. "What'd he give 'em?"

"Hell, I don't know — something with a needle. Something powerful."

"Probably ace," Dad said. "Ace promozine. There's not a thing I can do but take a look."

While Dad inspected a semiconscious steer's tongue, Deputy Dozel ran off with his bullhorn to organize the parade. The first car was the mayor's orange Cadillac, with steer horns fixed to the hood. Mayor Cox was a jowly, bossy fellow who liked to lead the way. Behind him came the unconscious longhorns, followed by us, the baton-twirling Rangerettes, six packs of Cub Scouts dragging flags, and several convertibles full of people who

thought they were important. The Merry Tigers marching band brought up the far rear, because they weren't
very good. Up front the mayor became impatient, looking
at his four-pound pocketwatch, and honked on his air
horn as a signal to start.

Dad came trotting back from the cattle. "I don't know
how much he gave them, but this'll be a damned slow
parade."

Sinclair had been scowling at the young posse. "Look at
them nitwits—not one remembered to bring cattle
prods."

Without Hot Shots the posse had to dismount and
punch and kick the beasts, who moved one step at a time.
By the time we turned onto Calhoun Street, Rose had
opened a can of Pearl; she'd thought the public shame and
humiliation would be over by now. I patted her knee and
looked back at Bengal. He seemed nervous, parading his
circus trailer; he wasn't used to being behind bars anymore.

But everything might have gone all right, if a freckle-
faced farmer's boy hadn't thrown the string of firecrackers
under Bengal's trailer. At first he only jumped around,
bouncing off the bars. But then he began to roar. It was
the sound of the first domino falling.

The drugged cattle in the rear heard him dimly. The
roar of a large jungle cat seemed to stir something in their
unconscious old blood. They began to shove clumsily
forward, frightening others.

"Slow down!" Dad hollered, and made a stab at Sinclair's brake pedal. Sinclair had been following closely,
nudging the straggling steers. Unfortunately Dad's foot

missed the brakes and hit the foot-feed. Sinclair whooped as we lurched into the herd.

A sluggish stampede ensued, with much mooing and scrambling of spectators. Behind us, frightened Bengal protected himself by roaring. The longhorns heard him, smelled him, and mushed forward. It may have been the first slow-motion stampede in history; and like a small boat in heavy surf, the mayor's Cadillac was caught up and carried away. All its occupants were screaming as they bore down on the Jaycee's bandstand.

Of course the band members saw the cattle and Cadillac coming, and one by one dropped their instruments and departed over the rail. The bandleader, however, did not. A disciplined little man, he kept his back turned and baton waving until the fat boy wiggled out of his tuba and jumped overboard. Then the bandleader turned. Shock lighted his face, and fear in liberal proportions.

I think the Cadillac must have hit the bandstand at just the right joint, because it came apart very quickly. Cattle trotted through the remains, scattering sheet music and stepping on musical instruments.

Meanwhile, Dad had found the brake pedal and stomped it. We were all pitched out of our lawnchairs, and Bengal's last roar ended with a whimper when he skidded to a stop on his chin. Then the Rangerettes behind us became confused. They'd been marching to the music until it stopped, and now as they watched the stampede, the batons from their high tosses were raining down on their heads. Several were immediately knocked unconscious, but most were simply dazed. They wandered among the confused horses of the unmounted posse, while Cub Scouts tried to pull them down for first aid. In the distance the bad Merry Tigers band honked and squeaked on their instruments.

"This didn't happen the way I expected," I said, helping the ladies untangle themselves from the lawn-chairs. Dad jumped out to help Claudine down, followed by lazy Sinclair. I gave Rose my hand. She seemed a little shaken.

"Are you all right?"

She nodded. "I'm fine. But you didn't need to throw yourself over me. We're enough of a spectacle as it is."

I tried to find some ray of hope as I helped her down from the truckbed. Off on the courthouse lawn the unmounted posse still chased the sluggish longhorns. The mayor shook his jowls at his bent Cadillac. The freckle-faced farmer's boy was being spanked without mercy. And somewhere the bandleader was weeping. Newspapers blew across the street and fallen bodies.

I gave Rose a hug as we looked at the mess. "I've heard it said that disaster brings people closer together."

She had to smile. Nearby, a gang of wounded, red-faced spectators in crushed hats weren't talking low when they cussed us. This disaster seemed more likely to *drive* us together. With an arm around Rose I reached through the trailer bars to comfort Bengal.

"You see to him," Rose said, brushing off her hands. "And I'll go help anybody who'll still let me."

Chapter
9

Busy as rose and i were avoiding foul mouthed townsfolk after that, we completely forgot about Shirley's surprise. Gradually it came to be the hot middle of July. On a torrentially rainy Thursday I spent the morning with the road crew hiding under the flatbed from the downpour. Finally at noon our pug-ugly foreman leaned out of the truck cab to empty his spit can. He acted surprised to see us.

"You boys — are you still under there? I thought I told you to go home."

It was only a half-mile run to our cars, and by the time I got there I was drenched. Naturally the De Soto didn't start. I had to catch a ride into town with little Johnny Boni, who'd recently bought his first car. In other people's cars he'd wanted to go fast, but in his own he only crept along. It was a '57 Chevy a grandmother had owned and permeated with her personality.

"Some car," Johnny said, bouncing on the seat. He was a short fellow and sort of fat, and he'd said the same thing a dozen times. "Some car."

He dropped me off at the Lone Star Cafe, where I wanted to kill some time. Actually, I wanted something good to eat; I'd seen Rose taking out leftover pea salad for tonight. In the far booth Randy was eating the blue plate and reading a letter.

"Another from Shirley?" I slid in. "You two must be in love."

"Shit," Randy grinned. He couldn't stay in love with a girl who wasn't near; he was too horny for that. He folded the letter up and sniffed at it, though. He wore an orange university tie.

"Where you been? I've been trying to get in touch with you."

Samantha, the undernourished waitress, interrupted us with my blue plate. Chicken fried steak, mashed potatoes, cream gravy and white bread — no vegetables because Alexander the constipated cook didn't believe in them. Samantha banged the plate down.

"That woman don't feed you enough. It's as plain as my face she don't."

No matter how short the conversation, Samantha always managed to point out her plain face. She huffed away.

"What's eating her?" I asked.

"Oh, you know Sam," Randy said. "She's angling for sympathy tips. But listen, I've been looking for you. Shirley keeps writing, asking if her mother's pregnant yet. Are you gonna throw away your shot at professional ball for —"

I put my fork down and butted in. "Did she mention how?"

Randy grinned. "I thought you knew how girls got pregnant."

"No, what I mean is, I mean —" but I didn't know what I meant. Randy didn't either, at first. He shook his head, then touched his earlobe thoughtfully.

"She did mention leaving a surprise in a diaphragm — some sort of crap like that."

"Could you be more specific?" I was leaning across the table. Randy was very particular about having his space violated by males. He pushed me back down.

"If she's not pregnant, just forget it and eat up. Two more weeks till we leave, and I want you feeling strong."

But I'd lost my appetite and felt weak jogging home. I brushed past Bengal in the dripping backyard and rushed inside to the bathroom. Rose's diaphragm resided there, in a little blue plastic house. I'd never really looked at it before; the diaphragm resembled a rubber turtle shell.

I held it up to the light and it seemed intact. But when I ran it full of tap water, the shell leaked in three or four places. Shirley must have poked a hat pin through it, several times. And Rose wouldn't have noticed, putting it on straight from the shower. I dried it carefully and put it back in its house. Then I sat down on the toilet and worried.

That evening after our run we lay out on the porch in the hammock I'd strung. Bengal pounced on sticks in the front yard, and the moist prairie breeze rattled the big pecan.

"Rose?"

"Hmm?" She lay with her head at my feet, relaxed and pleasantly exhausted. We'd run seven miles.

"Honey, I'm curious. When do you menstruate next?"
She sat up a little. "Not for a while. Are you feeling
waggish again?"

"No," I said. "Yes." I tried to act nonchalant. "I just like
to keep track of all your organs."

She lay back down, smiling between her feet at me. She
thought I was cutely ignorant of reproductive matters.

"Oh, in about two weeks. Toward the full moon. Mark
it on your calendar."

"I see," I said and grew thoughtfully silent. Rose may
have found it cute, but I felt stupidly ignorant of repro-
duction. I thought back to my sex education class. It had
been taught by Miss Salathe, who spent most of her time
avoiding embarrassing questions. She had shown us only
one movie — a cartoon about the penis and vagina. In it
happy sperm were represented by smiling tadpoles. They
paddled joyfully up some ovary canal. Happy eggs await-
ed them. I began to worry and to pray. I prayed that all
my sperm had been poor swimmers, and that all Rose's
eggs had had bad days.

Before we went to bed that night, Rose took a shower.
A bad omen. I quietly floated on our lily pad, thinking of
ways to injure Shirley. To top it all off, we'd gotten
another letter today.

Rose came in unfolding it and wearing a Merry Tigers
T-shirt and a towel around her hair. "I haven't read all of
it yet," she said, sitting on the edge of the bed. "This may
be the best part."

In this latest installment Lonny had started feeling
restless again, and La Vonne didn't like it one bit. She was
as possessive as she was vain. After his late nights out she

searched his clothing. One morning when Lonny was still asleep and the women were getting up for work, Shirley had caught La Vonne in his pants.

"Looking for something?" she said, with her as-if-I-don't-know smirk.

"Nothing for you to worry about, sugar." La Vonne found a matchbook and put it in her purse. "You just go ahead and eat your cereal. Maybe it'll make you grow."

Relations between the two had been warm, like friction, and Shirley said the condo seemed smaller and smaller each week. But it wasn't really a condo they lived in — rather a moderately shabby apartment complex. The Renters' Committee had only *talked* about converting, but La Vonne had airs. According to Shirley, La Vonne even mispronounced the word, making condominium sound like "something they put on a penis."

The new part of this long, detailed letter concerned the events of that night. Lonny came running in about midnight, while Shirley was doing homework by the light of TV. His shirttail was out and his hair unkempt. He ducked into the closet bar and poured himself a tall bourbon. He came out smoothing his hair.

"Daddy, what happened? Is she chasing you? That royal bitch!"

Lonny was shaken but Shirley's voice turned him to rage; it had that effect on men. "Damn right she is. The royalest bitch I ever met — excuse my language, sugar — but I was just sharing a booth with a friend, and she came in and shot off a gun. I could of wrung her neck."

"You should have," Shirley said, smelling blood and jumping up.

"Damn straight I should. Why, I'd like to kick her head. Damned bitch, shot a hole through the Budweiser clock."

Lonny was storming around the living room with Shirley behind. Then she thought of something, ran into the master bedroom, and returned with one of La Vonne's wigheads.

"You said you wanted to kick her head." She placed the wighead at her father's feet.

"Well, hell—" Lonny glared at the thing. "I believe I will."

Lonny kicked tar out of that wighead, and Shirley ran to get another. Within minutes they were punting wigheads all over the shabby living room and hollering like meat-eating savages.

" 'Then,' " Rose read aloud, " 'we heard La Vonne's key hit the lock. I don't know what got into Daddy, but he started blaming me. Naturally La Vonne believed him and now they've gone and grounded me for a month. As *if* I ever go anywhere but nite school. I haven't told you about that—I'm taking nite classes so I can graduate by X-mas—and get out of *everyone's* hair.

" 'All my disgust to Bubber. Temporarily yours, Shirley.' "

Rose folded up the letter and put it with the others in her bedside table. Then she snapped the light out and lay back.

"You're upset," I said.

"What gave you that idea?"

"Now don't get sarcastic," I said. "And don't worry. Shirley'll turn out all right."

135

Rose snorted when I said, "Don't worry," and moved a little away. I knew what she was thinking. She'd been selfish, sending her daughter away so she could have the summer with the ex-boyfriend. And now people in town stared at her, her daughter was living with people who shot at each other, and Lonny wasn't working, so Shirley wouldn't go to college. It all hadn't turned out too well.

For my part, I was worried about what Shirley had done. Poking holes in her mother's diaphragm! On top of everything else, it would hurt Rose too much.

A queen-sized bed can seem enormous when its occupants are full of regrets. Floating in bed in the darkness, it was as if we were lost in space. But neither of us wanted to be lost like that. Rose broke the silence first.

"Are you okay? You didn't finish your pea salad tonight."

"I'm fine. Just a little gas." I belched to prove it, and Rose slapped me in the arm. I reached up and took her hand. We must have lay like that for several hours, waiting for each other to go to sleep.

The next morning at Highland Drugs I fiddled around in the Stover Candy aisle until the shop cleared out of its early morning hypochondriacs. Old Mrs. Pritchett bought something to control the diarrhea yesterday's medicine had given her, and Mr. Spanks, the town drunk, ordered two bottles of Nyquil to go. My turn was next. Mr. MacDoogal, a barrel-chested Scot with a good stern laugh, was typing a prescription label. He'd been watching me, too, of course.

"What you need, son—some of these?" He reached under the counter for a package of lambskin Trojans. I guess I looked that kind of nervous.

"Uh, no, sir." I looked around to be sure the shop was empty. "I'll just take some of these Stress Tabs . . . and I need a diaphragm, too."

Mr. Mac lifted an eyebrow over his reading glasses. "You do?" He paused and decided to play along. "What size?"

I didn't know if Rose wore a small or medium. "Oh, one of each," I said. Mr. Mac waited. An explanation seemed in order. "I'm going on a binge."

Mr. Mac almost smiled. "That's a sixty, sixty-five, seventy, seventy-five—up to one-hundred centimeters. All-flex or Uni-form?"

The choices overwhelmed me.

"And, son, you need a prescription, too. Get one from your gynecologist."

I thought a moment. Mr. Mac went back to his typing. "Then I guess I'll just take these vitamins, and a tin of aspirin."

"You'd better make it Bufferin," he said. "You look a little sick to your stomach."

The only dishonest gynecologist I knew was Dr. Shorts, the sex fiend. Swallowing hard, I went to the hospital after work, creeping around the back stairs to avoid Rose's friends.

Dr. Shorts was lingering in the second-floor corridor, leaning over a heavyset nurse pressed to the wall. She was about forty-five and lantern-jawed like a lumberjack, but Dr. Shorts seemed very enamored.

"I've missed you, too," he was saying, "completely. And I've just got another week in this hellhole before I—"

"The answer's no. *N-O*. It took you two years to get around to me."

Dr. Shorts chucked her lantern chin. "I was saving the best till last."

"That's exactly what you told Sylvia last week. Can't you think up some new lines?" She ducked under his arm. "And don't think we divorced girls don't talk!"

Dr. Shorts watched her walk away, then shrugged, turned, and bumped into me. He stepped back quickly and looked me over. Was I somebody's husband?

"Don't I know you?"

"You might. We met once. You were using the same line on Rose Butts."

"Oh, yeah," he said, not remembering. "It works well with divorced women. Are you sure I don't know you?"

He seemed a little distracted, so I reminded him. "Rose Butts."

"Oh, yeah," he said absently, and started walking off. "Upstairs, in ortho."

I followed along.

"No, I wanted to see you — privately if I can. Man-to-man." I was afraid of being seen in the halls, knowing how divorced girls talked. Dr. Shorts kept walking.

"All right, all right, I was just gonna sack out anyway. Man talk, huh?"

We went to a small windowless medicine room, where the lazy doctor stretched out on an examining table. With his long hair and oval face, he resembled a well-fed, decadent Roman. He leaned up on one elbow, and laughed. "If this table could talk."

I laughed along with him; after all, I'd come asking favors. Dr. Shorts thought he was pretty funny.

"And what can I do for you? Need a D and C?"

I didn't understand the joke but it sounded dirty so I laughed heartily, feeling sick.

"I need a diaphragm."

He stopped laughing himself and gave me a look. "Hmm? What do you need it for?"

"A party hat," I said.

Dr. Shorts didn't recognize my attempt at humor. He rubbed his chin and thought. "Rose Butts," he said at last.

"It's not for her."

"Sure it isn't," he grinned, one scoundrel to another. "She's had a different look about her lately — I notice these things. And now that I think of it, she's rumored to be living with a tiger. That wouldn't be you, would it?"

"You sure don't let much get by you, Dr. Shorts."

He grinned again. "Don't kiss my ass. What size?"

I still didn't know.

"Hmm." He thought about it. "I'd eyeball her at an eighty — but take home as many as you want; I've only got another week left. Over there, the third cabinet."

By the time I'd stuffed my pockets with diaphragms galore, Dr. Shorts was snoring like a post-orgy Roman. I didn't wake him up to thank him, but I was thankful. A corrupt man in the right spot, it seemed, was a boon to all mankind.

The best laid plans of mice and men usually fail, though. After I flushed Shirley's surprise down the toilet, I roughed up a new one, size eighty, with soap and water and lodged it in its new home.

Later that night, after taking her shower, Rose groaned from the steamy bathroom. I quietly, and I hoped innocently, floated, until she came bustling in shaking a diaphragm. She had a very suspicious mind.

"Anything wrong, honey?"

"What is this?" She shook the thing loudly in my face.

"A diaphragm?"

"I know that — it's not mine." Her voice was taut. I sat up. I guess women get to know their diaphragms.

"Sit down," I said.

"Why?"

"Just sit down."

She did, rocking the waterbed. I looked at her before explaining. If I told her Shirley had revenged herself by poking holes in her diaphragm, she would be very hurt. This was a secret that must be kept. I decided to tell selected versions of the truth.

"I had to get you a new one. I flushed the old one down the toilet."

"Why?" She still didn't understand. "Why flush one, then buy another?"

"Rose, honey." I took her hand. "I was thinking about having babies, but I thought I ought to talk to you first."

"Babies?" she said. "Don't be absurd."

"I think it's a possibility," I said. "And what would you do if you accidentally got pregnant?"

She didn't need to think. "I'd have an abortion."

I must have looked hurt, worried, confused, and simpleminded, because she took extra time with me. "Look, Bubber, I've already had my family. I don't want any more children. I feel great now. I'm running, I'm not smoking or drinking, I wake up in the morning feeling fresh. I'm even running a race next week." She lay a warm hand on my cheek and kissed my cowlick. "I probably haven't thanked you enough for all you've done, but I mean it. Thanks."

Her appreciation seemed sincere, but it wasn't enough.

"Then you definitely won't marry me?"

She laughed and kissed me again. "I've already married one nineteen-year-old."

"But he was a jerk."

She looked over at me, then snapped out the bedside light. Even in the half-light of the moon-filled window, I could see her expression soften. "That's right. And you're not a jerk," she said. "But you *are* only nineteen."

Chapter

10

THAT WEEKEND CLAUDINE MOVED INTO THE serpentarium under unclear circumstances. All the time we were unloading Sinclair's truck she kept saying she didn't know how long she'd be staying, but at least until they finished painting her house.

"It never needed no paint," Sinclair groused from under the weight of a small table lamp. It was the first thing he'd carried all day; he claimed his arthritis had kicked up.

"Very convenient," Dad said, "your lameness."

"Hell, Dad —" I passed him with a sofa on my head, "you haven't carried much more."

"I'm supervising," he said. "I know where everything's supposed to go."

Which was a lot of horseflowers, too. Dad, the hypocrite, maintained that Claudine would occupy my old room ("now that you ran off to live in sin") and he even made me carry her double-spring, double bed up the stairs. The mattress couldn't have weighed less than a car.

And in the end it appeared that Claudine had too much of everything, anyway. The house now had two of all. Two refrigerators, two kitchen tables, two massive photo albums. It was two entire existences, head to head. In the areas with breathing space, we had to walk around sideways, and even Loops, who normally liked tight dark places, found the house too much a jumble. Clearly life was not possible here anymore. Loops bumped open the kitchen door and oozed away down the back steps. Claudine followed, followed by Dad, and outside by the butane tank they stopped to argue. Each of us, in our way, had worked hard, and we were tired and tempers were thin. Sinclair went to one of the refrigerators and tried to find beer, while I stood up in the kitchen where I used to sit. Sounds of the argument drifted in.

"I told you to bring a *few* things."

"Don't scold me, Charlie Drumm. Your place always looked larger to me."

"But you could of thought —"

"I did," she said, "and I was wrong. But what are we gonna do about it now? I can't just throw it all away."

"I didn't say *all*. Just some. I've got plenty of furniture myself."

"Plenty of what? Beat up old chairs? A wood stove? We'd be better off tossing those."

"Now Claudine, some of those things are priceless heirlooms. And a lot of memories are attached to those things. Why, I remember the first time I ever burned myself — it was on that Windsor wood stove."

"Well," Claudine replied, "I'm only ten years behind

you in memories. And I'm too old to tote wood for a stove."

An impasse had been reached, and neither side would budge. Inside the kitchen Sinclair moaned over his beer. "I know exactly what's gonna happen next. We're gonna have to carry it all back. Go on out there, Bubber, see if you can patch this up."

I opened the screen door tentatively. Both parties still looked grumpy. Claudine was shedding skin off of Loops's back, and Dad was staring out across the waving fields of rice. They both seemed to be reconsidering the new order of things. Past a certain age, maybe people were too set in their ways to move in together. But neither of them was happy alone. They probably would have gotten married, but then their Social Security would be cut in half.

"Uh," I said to break the silence. "Uh, I couldn't help overhearing, what with my big ears. May I make a suggestion?"

Claudine looked at me first. She liked me at least enough to listen. Gradually Dad turned his ear toward me, too.

"You both have too much furniture, right? And each piece has some sort of precious memory. Well, why don't you each throw away half your memories? That's the modern thing to do."

When I spoke, they seemed to listen. I stepped back inside to let them consider, and bumped into eavesdropping Sinclair.

"Great," he grumbled, "now you've gone and done it.

We'll *still* have to carry a full load to the dump. It's what I get, I suppose, for asking the son of a mule to help out."

The Houston 10,000 began at seven on our last Saturday, so we got up early, dressed in the dark, and drove to Houston submerged in silent thoughts. My situation in life had grown more complicated. Rose had found some blood on her underwear (don't ask me how I know, but I know) and she'd decided she was menstruating. However, she'd also thrown up this morning. What could this mean? Nerves, she'd said when I pounded on the bathroom door. I suppose I believed her, but a woman's body is a baffling thing. Add to this uncertainty, the day after tomorrow I was leaving for college, and I was a worried man. Brooding, I reached over absently and sipped from Rose's coffee.

"Ah, honey," I finally said. "You know I don't want you to feel tied down when I'm gone. Just do whatever you want."

Rose, who'd been sipping contemplatively, looked up skeptically. "You don't mean that."

"No, of course I don't. I just thought I ought to say it; you've told it to me often enough."

She smiled. "But *I* meant it. Now be quiet and think about the race."

The race was 10,000 meters — how far that meant in miles I didn't know because I didn't ask. Physically I was in good shape for a ballplayer, which meant little or nothing on the long-distance course. My pack of muscles felt heavy, and I'd never seen so many slender city people, doing stretching exercises under the rising sun. For a while I wandered around gazing at the surroundings and trying to find a bathroom. The coffee had gone directly to my bowels.

Nearby, on the tennis courts, relaxed people in whites smacked Day-Glo balls back and forth, before the summer heat and humidity got too bad, and out on the golf course the dewy fairways were already streaked by the shoes and carts of morning golfers. A gentle breeze tossled the huge pines and water oaks, and the light traffic on the freeway made a pleasant, friendly sound. There were no bathrooms, however.

Rose flagged me down as I trotted past with pinched cheeks. "What's the matter? Your face looks funny."

"Diarrhea."

"You have it?"

"I want to, but I can't find a big enough tree."

She pinned a number on my back, and a group of lean young women jogged past, their eyes detached and inward looking. I was about to mention this when I noticed Rose's own detached and inward gaze. Ahead of her on the 10,000 meters lay more pain than she was used to. And ahead of me lay, I hoped, a big, private tree. A huge mass of runners were bunching up at the starting line and we joined them.

"I'll stay with you as long as I can," I said, low, but an older, sinewy man beside me thought I was talking to him.

"Just run your own race, Sonny. That's all anyone can do."

When the gun went off the whole herd started moving. It was immediate chaos and I soon lost Rose. From time to time I could see her red head of hair bobbing farther and farther ahead of me, as I sank farther back in the pack. My muscles felt suddenly ungainly and unnecessary, and I noticed with much pain all the smaller fellows zipping past. I told myself that the reason I was slow was that I had to run with my cheeks together.

After an unbearable length of time I saw my dream tree ahead. A truly magnificent old water oak. I ran behind it, fertilized it, and entered the race again. Shortly after this I passed the first mile marker and became extremely depressed. How many more miles to go?

Passing the five-mile marker I couldn't see Rose anymore and found myself pacing with a tall black fellow wearing ordinary tennis shoes. After a mile or so of panting together he looked over and said:

"I don't know."

"I don't know either," I wheezed.

After that the race began to resemble a forced march. Victims fell off to the side, clutching various parts of their painful bodies. I didn't know who I was running with anymore. I concentrated only on my body. Which valuable part of me would snap first?

I think I lost contact with reality sometime then. My feet slapped, my lungs filled and expelled, but I can't describe more than that. I remember a dozen onlookers clapping and shouting encouragement, but my vision was strange and their faces looked stretched. All I knew was that Rose was somewhere ahead.

Then I heard her voice, very near — in my ear to be exact. A remarkable likeness of her seemed to be running beside me.

"Bubber, Bubber," this vision said. "You can stop running now."

Apparently it was an evil vision, intent on making me quit. I shrugged it off and kept plugging. So did it.

"Mr. Persistence," it said. "You've passed the finish line."

When it grabbed my arm firmly, I stopped. Rose led me to some pyracantha bushes where I threw up.

"How'd you do?" I bubbled.

"Great. Really great."

I straightened up and looked at her with watery eyes. She did look good, her bushy hair tied back with a green sweatband, and her T-shirt soaked with good sweat.

"Sorry I couldn't stay with you." I ducked down quickly again.

She smiled and waited. Then she towed me to the car. I couldn't have found it myself. "You're just not in your prime yet," she said. "I think I'd better drive."

That night at home she felt less great but still good. I couldn't believe she was older than me. I lay semiconscious on the sofa with both feet in a tub of Epsom salts, while Rose talked about the race and brushed off her shoes. She seemed even more fond of those blue New Balances. She stayed up until twelve-thirty watching the Late Show — *Harvey*, starring Jimmy Stewart — and then she woke me and guided me back to the waterbed. No man, it seemed, was ever tended by a finer woman.

Book III

Chapter

11

COLLEGE BEGAN FOR ME WITH TWO-A-DAY WORK-
outs in the stinging heat of August. Between practices I
took salt tablets and napped, dreaming uncomfortably
about our freshman coaches. They were the most disciplined mean men I'd ever met, but I guess they had to be.
Every year they started from scratch with a bunch of boys
like me, who thought football was fun. It had been, back
at Merry High; a spirited game where friends from one
little town blocked and tackled friends from another, to
the lusty cheering of fans. If we won we were happy all
night; if we lost we consoled ourselves in the arms of
sympathetic girlfriends.

But college coaches had less sympathy. The university
had spent a fortune giving scholarships to three times as
many boys as it needed. The freshman coaches' job was to
weed out the best, and run the broken losers off in
disgrace. And the trick was to get the scholarships back, so
no losers could ride the gravy train. The coaches made
these crucial decisions based on minute observation, not

only of our ability on the field, but on some essential ingredient called "Attitude."

But that's not to say that these men, who controlled our futures, were intelligent. My offensive line coach, for instance, was slightly smarter than a short stick. Coach Grimes was his name, a devout reborn Christian with close-cropped brown hair and a university ballcap permanently forced on his overweight forehead. He resembled President Taft, in the back of the neck. I doubt he could write more than three or four words in the English language, but he was expert at detecting Attitude.

Every afternoon after the late workout Coach called us all around him. We were sweat-soaked and bruised along every bone, but being this close to a coach recharged us. When he blew his whistle we ran in place growling, snorting, snarling, grunting, spitting — doing anything to make him believe we could crush all opponents with an animal smile. My growls were particularly impressive, because I'd had the advantage of growing up with Bengal.

One afternoon Coach's dumb eyes came to rest on me. I was jumping and flailing like a tiger eating a jungle village. Coach Grimes seemed to approve.

"THAT A WAY!" Coach always spoke at the top of his lungs, to show his Attitude, too. "WHERE'D YOU GET THAT LEG SCAR, DRUMM?"

"My tiger, sir!" I hollered back, managing to let loose with an explosive string of farts. "Got it wrestling my tiger!"

"GOOD, GOOD! HE EAT YOUR EAR LOOSE TOO?"

"No, Sir! A street fight, sir!"

"THAT A BOY! KEEP FARTING! HUBBA, HUBBA!" Excited, Coach hit me twice with his whistle chain, a sign of affection on the gridiron.

Naturally I called Rose every night, except weekends when I called twice a day. Many times, *too* many times, Rose wasn't there. When I asked where she'd been, she just laughed. Which meant she'd been out with other men. To say that I missed her was wrong; I felt I'd left the most important part of my chest back in her house. On the tiny desk in my dorm room I kept a framed picture of her and Bengal running. Bengal had been moved back to his cage between the gas pumps; Rose visited him on her way home from work, and sometimes she ate supper with Dad and Claudine.

One evening at the end of August, Rose was home the first time I called. She was cleaning house, she said, because Shirley was coming home.

"Her letter says Lonny got shot. It's not bàd, in the leg. He claims La Vonne did it, but she says he shot himself so he wouldn't have to work. I don't know who to believe. Anyway, I've ordered Shirley home. I don't want her killed in a jealous gunbattle."

"Good idea," I said. "But check her at the door. She might be armed herself."

Rose laughed. "She'll be all right. And I'll be glad to have her here." She paused a moment. "And Bubber, I'd appreciate it if you wouldn't call so much. If I'm not here, she'll answer the phone and say things we'll both regret."

"But," I said, "but I left her the De Soto. Maybe she'll like that."

At the other end of the line I could feel Rose smiling, thinking about her little girl. "Shirley can't be bribed, you know that." She paused again and thought of something else. "And I don't want what happens here to affect you up there. You're in college, don't waste it."

"Sure," I said lamely. "I'll go out with three girls a night if it'll make you happy."

"Believe it or not," she said, "it would."

After we said a few more things that didn't fill my hollow chest, I went upstairs to my room. My roommate, Ruby Jones, was on his bed slamming his head between two books. Ruby, who filled the door to its jambs, was a twenty-four-year-old who'd played tackle for the prison team. Someone noticed him and told someone else, and eventually he got a college scholarship. The only problem was that Ruby couldn't read. He liked college, though; the girls were long-legged and the food better than at Huntsville. He liked it enough to want to stay, and to do that he had to make the team. So he used his textbooks as best he could, banging them against his head. The day I moved in he'd explained his strategy. "Nerves — got to pound them out. They's what make you hurt."

Tonight he looked up and said, "You got it, man."

"What?" I sat down on my lonely bed, looked at the poster I'd put over it — showing a hairy Cro-Magnon man dragging a tree limb — and picked up a heavy chemistry book.

"The position, man. Coach likes your growls."

"I'm pretty good on the field, too."

"She-it! The growls is what matter."

Ruby went back to slamming his head methodically. I watched him for a while, and then I started hitting my chest with the chemistry book. By the time I was a junior, I figured, I'd have most of the feeling pounded out.

Ruby was right about one thing. The morning the roster came out, I was playing first string right guard. Randy, who'd slept through his morning classes, too, came down to the team bulletin board with me. He searched for his name and found he'd been shifted from quarterback to wide receiver, third string. He was mad about it.

"Dad'll kill me, and it's not fair. I spent all summer memorizing plays in the storeroom, and you didn't even crack the book."

I couldn't resist kidding him, polishing my nails. "Natural ability, I guess."

"Shit, don't get cocky yet. This roster doesn't mean a thing — only now the varsity knows whose joints they're gonna separate. They're eating meat tonight, for the scrimmage tomorrow."

And that night at the training table the varsity did make our lives miserable. They wanted us thoroughly intimidated for tomorrow. In practical terms this meant they threw steakbones at us. They took away our chairs, too, so we had to eat on the floor. And after dinner they lined us up against the wall, and faced us down man-to-man, the way we'd face tomorrow.

My defensive guard was large, to say the least. He wore shorts to show his oak-post calves. He hadn't finished chewing his dinner, and from the size of the lump in his cheek he'd be lucky to finish by bedtime. I stared at him. He didn't have any front teeth.

"My mama walked me with a leash," he said. "And I eat glass."

I believed he did, but I was too scared to speak. He took my silence for skepticism. Turning around, he whipped up a milk glass and began biting it. I saw his technique — chew the glass into small fragments, then swallow it with a little dough from his cheeks. It seemed a good technique, but his empty gums still bled.

"I hate you," he said.

"I'm sorry," I said.

"I'm gonna bust you open like a feed sack."

"Yes, sir!"

"And then I'm gonna pick my teeth with your ribs."

"Good, sir!"

He chewed some more glass contemplatively, like a cow. "You're a smart-ass, but it ain't gonna do you any good."

"No, sir!"

"Which arm you want broke?"

"My left, I guess."

"Which leg?"

"Either one," I said. Both of them were shaking.

"You got any calls to make, better do it tonight."

Outside the training table a sort of animal frenzy had broken loose. Varsity linemen crouched, facing the cinderblock wall. When the center yelled "Hup!" they all crashed into it, smacking their forearms against the concrete. They hit it so hard that the phone in the booth jingled. I sneaked over to it and dialed Rose. To get out of the public eye, I slid down in the booth. Shirley answered and recognized my voice.

"You bastard!"

"Now, Shirley."

"You son of a bitch bastard! You know what you did?"

I knew several things, all of which would infuriate her. I remained carefully quiet.

"You impregnated my mother!"

"I what?"

"You heard me. My mother, the unwed mother."

"Are you sure?"

"Ha! The home pregnancy test is right here on the kitchen table."

"But how?"

"Ha! again."

The punctured diaphragm, of course. After the initial shock, I got mad. "You had as much to do with it as me." I spoke hotly. "I discovered your surprise."

Now Shirley became silent. In a smaller voice she asked, "Does Momma know?"

"She might, if you don't behave."

"Harumpf!" she spat. "That's blackmail."

"Don't talk to your future stepfather like that."

I heard her teeth grinding before she slammed down the phone. I rose up to dial again. My opponent of tomorrow stalked past, still chewing on the milk glass. I slid back down. Rose answered.

"Is it true?"

She said nothing, or yes.

"Why didn't you tell me?"

Nothing again.

"Talk to me. What are we going to do?"

When she spoke I wished she hadn't. "*You* aren't doing anything. *I'm* going to the Emma Goldman Clinic tomorrow."

"Not without me, you're not. And I want you to know, I'm against abortion."

"I thought you would be. What's that noise?"

The linebackers were still beating the nerves out of their forearms. It was like calling from the front lines.

"Nothing — just some boys studying hard."

Rose's voice was sad. "Well, that's what I want you to do. You've got your whole future to think of; what happens back here shouldn't affect you."

I was quiet a moment, my hand over the receiver so she wouldn't hear the cussing. Several linebackers were bleeding and they were yelping happily. Tomorrow it would be somebody else's blood.

"Rose, honey, you're not talking to Lonny. What happens to you *does* affect me. I'll be there in the morning; I'm going with you, at least."

"Bubber, I —"

"Don't say another word. I'll behave, I promise."

"I doubt that very much," she said, and paused. "But I'd appreciate the company. The only thing I can't understand is how. I was so careful."

From Rose's kitchen I heard Shirley holler, "*I'll* tell you how, Momma," and Rose tenderly hung up the telephone. I guess Shirley couldn't be bribed *or* blackmailed.

Upstairs I found Randy in his room putting black smears under his eyes with a burnt cork. He was seeing how he looked as a wide receiver, I guess. After I explained my situation to him, he put the cork down.

"God, you really fucked up."

"That's not what I need right now. I need your car, for all day tomorrow."

"My car? My Bonneville convertible? You mean you're gonna miss the scrimmage?"

"I guess so. And I'm not too sorry about it either."

Down the hall a marauding gang of varsity monsters were setting fire to the freshman quarterback's door. We listened to the screams from within — within us, that is.

"All right." Randy fumbled for his keys. Before he handed them over he said, "You'll probably be on the Third String Shit List with me now — so just remember who lent you his car."

Chapter 12

I'D ALREADY FORGOTTEN HOW BEAUTIFUL THE prairie was in September, the rice fields cut to stubble and the early geese floating out above them. The summer harvest must have been plentiful, because passing through town I saw many new pickups, and atop a new tractor Mr. Jim Darrow dickered with the John Deere salesman. Likewise, Rose's pecan had done very well; I parked under its nut-laden boughs.

Rose heard me and came out snarling. She dumped herself into the Bonneville wearing new Levi's and a green cowl neck, and without a word began beating me with a huge leather purse. She grunted with pleasure delivering each blow; evidently Shirley had told her all. I took my punishment placidly, like an ox who's stepped on his master's toe.

"You and Shirley, *ugh!* Love games with my body, *ugh!*"

"You don't believe that, ooof! I love you, ooof, ooof!"

"Love? *Ugh!*"

"Yes. Ooof!"

Resting her arm, Rose searched through the purse with a shaky hand and drew out a cigarette. A Marlboro, slightly crooked from colliding with my head. She lit it in a determined manner, intent on harming *both* the bodies that had betrayed her, hers and mine.

I couldn't sit idly by. "Don't you know what that thing does to your lungs?"

"My lungs? *Umph!*" Her purse crashed down on my cowlick. Somehow I put the big car in gear and launched it dizzily onto the ranch road. The pummeling continued almost to the Interstate, but the worst seemed over now. That is, I began to go numb above the neck.

But Rose looked lovely, beating me. Her dense hair, even longer now, shook loose from its beret; her freckles darkened with anger. And in her Levi's she didn't show yet, but she seemed to. I wondered about the effect of this beating on our little fetus. I hoped it didn't have ears yet, what with Rose cussing like never before.

"Son of a bitch! Bastard! Fuckermother!"

"That's motherfucker, honey."

"*Uggh!*"

At the freeway ramp she threw her purse down, growling, and drew out another cigarette.

"Keep your eyes on the road, not me. We don't need another accident."

I drove down the highway a little. She seemed exhausted, spent.

"Don't you think we ought to discuss this thing, like adults?"

Rose summoned up a voice most people use to spit with. "Do you think you can? After all, you're not."

She could be venomous at times. I drove on, feeling snake-bitten and extremely disappointed. We should have been much happier. My own parents had tried for years to have the same kind of accident. I thought about my mother, and how overjoyed she would have been. She'd loved children, especially unplanned ones which seemed extra-special gifts, and she'd passed that love on to me. Perhaps if I explained my feelings?

"Look, honey, there's a bright side to this."

"I'm sure."

"No, really. We could have this baby."

"Correction: *I* could have it. It's *my* body, remember?"

"But I'm the father," I argued.

"Correction again: you and Shirley shared jointly in that."

"Well, correct me in this —" I reached for her hand, which she withdrew to her lap. "We're in love. Now there's a baby on the way, and we ought to make it right." I paused. "You see how simple it is?"

Rose used her long-distance-spitting voice: "I see how simple *you* are. Maybe you *are* a moron."

I must have looked brutalized — I know I felt it — and gradually Rose heard what she'd spat. Her jutted chin lowered a notch; with reluctance she glanced at me, my open can cowlick, my foolishly drooping ear. I tried to look attractively crushed. She slumped a little in the seat, sighing. It was no use hating me.

"Sorry. I didn't mean that. But your feelings don't change a thing. You don't believe in abortion — I'm not raving about it myself. But I've already had my family, and in a million years I wouldn't start over." She paused and looked out at the passing rice fields. A few geese were landing, and a few were taking off. She'd come a long way, only to get pregnant.

I reached over and comfortably took her hand. We drove along commiserating with our fingers. But I wasn't going to give up. I loved this woman; she was plump with my fetus. I glanced at her sideways.

"I'm taking that anthropology course, like you told me to. We're reading about the African Bushmen."

Rose perked up a bit. She liked to read about primitive tribes; as a girl she'd wanted to be a medical missionary, like Dr. Schweitzer.

"The Bushmen? The short ones?"

I nodded. "They've got a tight, strong society. And for them, nineteen's real old for fatherhood."

Rose squeezed my fingers, amused but unswayed. "Well, for you it's too young. You haven't even grown into your ears yet. And we both have our futures to think of."

The Emma Goldman Clinic lay in the West University district, a neighborhood of enlightened city people. Elderly bearded oaks shaded large old houses and small efficient cars. Here and there a house had been converted into a doctor's office or antique store. The clinic itself was a two-story brick mansion with many chimneys. And it might have been a nice place, but we arrived on a bad day. As we came up the walk a frightened young woman rushed down the steps, followed by her heavyset father.

"Evelyn! Evelyn!" he called after her. She jumped into

his car and locked all the doors. Her father spoke through the vent window. "He's a bum. You're throwing your life away. Please, *please* come back inside."

I turned to Rose at the steps. "Another satisfied customer?"

She had to smile. "One of many, I'm sure. Now come on and don't cause trouble. This is supposed to be serious."

If she hadn't mentioned seriousness I would have noticed it in Emma Goldman's. Abortion clinics are not normally habitated by exuberant animals, but I'm sure the real Emma Goldman had a better sense of humor than the rational women who worked in her name. The first one we met was the receptionist — at least I guess that's who she was. She stood nearest the phone on the floor of the absolutely bare waiting room. There was no furniture in it at all.

"Gypsies stole everything," she said. She wore her hair in an extremely tight bun and seemed stunned by the pain it must have caused her.

We were joined by a woman administrator in a three-piece suit and necktie. She spoke to Rose. "One of their princesses was here yesterday, to terminate a problem pregnancy. The king didn't approve."

"Gypsies stole everything," the receptionist said again. On second glance there was an expression in her eyes that said, No one at home inside. Instinctively, Rose reached out to help, but the administrator drew her quickly aside.

"Adelle's not at the sharing stage of her Post-Theft Trauma yet. Luckily several of us in Group have been raped, and we're going to get behind her experience tonight. We're better prepared, don't you think?" She led Rose farther away, as if to shelter Adelle from an unmolested woman. "Now if you'll just take a place we'll fill out your forms in a moment. We're running a little behind."

We found a place against the wall, where the end of the line seemed to be. About a dozen other women waited, as if for a bus. I leaned over to whisper:

"Are you sure this is the place? I don't hear any blood-curdling screams."

"Shh! And behave yourself." Rose looked uncomfortably around. My presence had attracted unwanted attention; I was the only man in the abortion line. The staff glanced sharply at me as they passed through; they seemed to hold me responsible for every unwanted pregnancy in the room. To avoid their eyes I pretended to examine a wall poster the Gypsies hadn't stolen. Apparently it wasn't to their tastes. It showed a convention of angry women shaking their fists at the camera. The caption read, "Sisters United: E.R.A. N.O.W.!"

Neither Rose nor I had any qualms with the clinic's politics — certainly women should be treated equally — but Rose wasn't as absolutely confident she was right as the staff seemed to be. Marching across the room's bare hardwood floors, their footsteps sounded martial. Rose stirred uneasily at my side. She'd made her share of mistakes, the biggest of which was me.

"A moment" must be universal hospital jargon for two hours. Waiting on alternate feet we eavesdropped on the girl in front of us, as the counsellor wrote on a clipboard. The girl, about my age, had mousy hair and the lively imagination of the inbred or feebleminded. She came from a mediocre town in East Texas and spoke with a twang.

"Father's occupation?" the counsellor asked.

"Oh, Daddy? He's a cedar whacker, when he works."

"A . . . cedar whacker?"

"Sure, you know, he chops down trees for fenceposts. That's all we can grow on the farm—that and blisters."

"I see. And is he willing or able to contribute to the cost of the termination?"

"Daddy? Heck, he didn't impregnate me. An alien did it."

"An alien?"

"Sure, you know—one of them visitors from the Planet Mars. He was dressed up to look like my boyfriend, but I knew it wasn't him. Sonny never acted like that in his life. And he swore he was playing pool, all eight times."

"I see," the counsellor said, very understanding. She seemed to have run across many alien impregnations; they were fairly common in East Texas. She directed the girl down the hall, where she'd be counseled and tested further, and then she stepped up to Rose.

Apparently it was better to consort with an alien than with me; the counsellor gave me the coolest of scans. Sore-footed, I was leaning against the wall and the wall poster. She told me to get off.

"No disrespect, ma'am," I said. "I believe everyone should have the right to be a woman."

My attempt at humor failed. The counsellor raised her eyebrows and pushed up her granny glasses. Rose stirred uneasily again; she was used to being on the other side of the clipboard, and like most people who dispensed help, she was lousy at receiving it. She answered in an abrupt manner.

"Marital status?"

"Single."

"Occupation?"

"Registered nurse."

The counsellor looked up. She'd had a long day already and her granny glasses seemed to pinch her nose. She'd probably asked herself a hundred times this morning how *so* many women got pregnant. She decided to take it out on Rose. "Then as a nurse you're familiar with the means of birth control?"

"I am." No further comment.

"Religion?"

"Catholic — or I was."

"Oh, I see." A pause. "The man's name is not required, of course."

"Well, I'm him," I interjected. "Bubber Drumm with two *m*'s. A native of the Planet Earth."

The counsellor gave me a cool eye, as if she doubted it. Her variety of Earthlings didn't joke, have loose ears, or wantonly sow their irresponsible seeds. I tried to improve my standing.

"But in our relationship Rose doesn't shave her legs, and I'm the weak, subservient one."

"I see," she said, dismissing me as a goofball. "And you want him present at the consultation?"

This seemed dubious to her, which made me tight. Goofball or not, I was the father-not-to-be; I had some rights.

"If there's a space on your form for this, write it down: I'm stuck on this woman like her hair."

Smiling, Rose struck me in the ribs with her elbow. "He's only partially responsible. My daughter had a hand in it, too — but she's home recuperating from a bout with a hairbrush."

"Your daughter?" The woman looked us over again. A thirty-five-year-old redhead, a younger big-eared Earthling? A hairbrush? What sort of perverts were we? Her expression wavered on the edge of disapproval, but duty soon took command again. She sent us down the hall, the sixth door on the right.

I stopped Rose in the hall. "Honey, this may be our last chance to talk alone. I want you to know that I'm sorry. I feel responsible for all this, and I have to say this isn't the responsible thing to do."

Rose looked up. "Maybe not — but don't apologize. It's my own fault for not behaving right." She paused, absorbing the blame herself. "But if you don't feel good about this, maybe you should wait in the car."

"No," I said. "I belong here. I'm the man."

Strange to say, but these words made me feel precariously on the edge of manhood, which felt like the edge of a steep cliff. Rose looked down and thought, before she pushed me off that cliff.

"You might not be."

"What do you mean?"

"Just that — you might not be the father."

She was avoiding my eyes.

"Oh, God," I groaned. "You've been fooling around?"

Rose had no comment.

"I don't believe you. You're just taking the pressure off me, right?"

Rose turned quickly to avoid the question, and opened the wrong office door. It was already occupied by a blonde weeping in a folding chair and a brawny fellow standing over her.

"Oh, I'm sorry," Rose said, stepping back.

The brawny fellow looked up. He had one massive eyebrow and spoke in a deep voice. "Where'd that counsellor go? There should have been Kleenex in the office."

"Can I help?" Rose dipped into her purse for some tissue. The woman sobbed freely into them.

"It's all right, Marcia." The big fellow patted her shoulder with a hairy hand. His wife was a very pretty woman. Tall, with slim hips and yellow hair curled up in front. Very tan, too, even to the fingertips. Her husband was saying, "You're right. I'm wrong. What else do you want me to say?" His beautiful wife's tears affected him tremendously.

"Nothing," she said, "nothing, nothing."

Rose went to her side. "What's the trouble? Is there anything I can do?" At work she was used to comforting people and she felt most comfortable doing it. Marcia looked up and gauged her.

"All I want's an abortion. Ronny doesn't, but it's not *his* body."

Rose sat down on the other folding chair, with Ronny watching her. He was a hairy, masculine guy, with a pelt growing out his shirt collar, but he had uncommonly soft brown eyes.

"Marcia's worried about looking like her mother. Mrs. Margolis was once a Miss Texas."

"That's not it completely," Marcia moaned. "I'm just not *ready* for children. I need to *live* a little first."

"But darling, people with children are still alive."

"Not like I want to be," Marcia said. "It's fine for you; you get to keep your job. But I'd be so swollen I couldn't go outside."

"Are you afraid of pregnancy?" Rose asked.

Marcia looked at her, woman to woman. "A little," she admitted. "That thing — that little thing — attached inside of me." She shivered. "And I'm sick of feeling weak and throwing up. If Ronny wants this thing so much, let *him* have it."

"But darling," Ronny said, "I can't."

"Well, I can't either. I'm not going to throw away my future in real estate because of your inadequacies."

Ronny shook his head. They'd obviously argued it through before. "Okay, all right. I don't want you to throw up. But let's just get this thing over with."

I'd been listening impatiently over his shoulder, which I tapped. "Hey, mine uses the same argument with me, but don't give up. It's not just their lives anymore. You have to fight for your fetus."

"Who are you?" Marcia snapped.

"Be quiet," Rose said, losing her patience, too. "You've got to have better reasons than those. Keep trying, Ronny."

Poor Ronny looked a little bewildered, getting so much advice. Marcia had always won this argument. She intended to continue the trend.

"What you're all forgetting is that it's *my* future, and *my* body. And *I* want the thing taken out."

Rose sat back, astonished by Marcia's single-minded devotion to her body, and she seemed to choose her words with care, restraining an outburst. "But it's not just *your* body anymore. This decision you're making, it can't be that self-centered."

I'd never heard Rose talk like that before, and I looked down at her. When we'd entered the room she'd been ready to have an abortion. But seeing Marcia wearing her argument had made her own seem underdressed.

Marcia was aghast, but sarcastic. "And I guess you're here for a dental appointment? Who do you think you are, anyway?"

"Rose Butts." Rose stood up with the air of resolution. "I've been a mother before, and now I'm pregnant again."

"Yes, well, we can see you're not wearing a wedding ring, can't we, Ronny?"

"Actually," I lied to protect Rose's credibility, "Ms. Butts is here with a surgical inspection team. She's a nurse and I'm an exterminator."

"That's right." Rose gathered her purse. "And this clinic is filthy. Gypsies ransacked it and left a colony of body lice. You'd better leave, too, Marcia — I know how you feel about parasites."

Outside the clinic I tried to embrace Rose, to celebrate her momentous decision, but she pushed me away. "Give me the keys. I want to drive this big car."

On the freeway I made another attempt. "We really have to get married now. Even if you were fooling around, I'm the most-probable-father-to-be."

She smiled at my terminology. "Oh, no. Not back to square one. You're going back to college, and I'm going to act like nothing's the matter, until I have this little body louse. As for us, we're not seeing each other anymore. Enough damage has been done. And I *mean* it."

Steering the long-nosed Bonneville through traffic, she spoke with a resolute jut to her chin, a ship's captain in a stormy sea. She was taking the helm and she knew she could handle it, alone. After all, she'd finished 10,000 meters at a run. And it was her body.

That evening I told Dad he was a most-probable-grandfather-to-be. He and Claudine were at the kitchen table with Pierce and Magnolia, the house-rats.

"A granddad. Hot durn!" Overjoyed, he hugged Claudine, then me, then Claudine several more times. Gradually, though, his spirits and bushy eyebrows sank. He'd realized something out of the ordinary here.

"A *most-probable*-grandpa-to-be?"

"That's right. We're not exactly sure who's the man."

Dad sat down. "Can't we be sure of *any*thing anymore? I don't suppose you're married or anything like that."

"No."

"So, I'm an illegitimate most-probable-grandfather-to-be?" Dad clasped his head. "Who's the mother? Do you even know her?"

"It's Rose," Claudine said, "you dimwitted old vet." She smiled up at me. "We've got real fond of her stopping by for supper."

"Well, you'll see a lot more of her than I will. I stopped

off at Highland Drugs and bought these vitamins. Be sure she takes them, okay?"

"Durn right we will," Dad muttered. "We don't want that baby turning out like you. An illegitimate most-probable-grandpa-to-be?" He was still trying to pierce the complications.

"When?" Claudine asked.

"March. The middle."

"That soon?" she said. "I'll start knitting tomorrow."

"Knit pink!" Dad said getting excited again. After all, a baby was being born with remote connections to him. "Knit pink! We'll name her Abby after her illegitimate most-probable-grandma."

"That'd be sweet," Claudine said. "But if it's a girl, I hope it favors Rose. You two boys'd make real homely girls."

After a good Claudine-style Bohemian sausage dinner, Dad walked me out to the Bonneville, belching softly. I stopped to scratch Bengal through the bars. He was partially asleep, like most caged wild animals.

"He's getting lazy again," Dad said. "But mean this time."

"He'll get over it."

"I don't think so. You gave him too much freedom too soon. In the morning he just gnaws on those bars." Dad paused, watching me in the shrewd way he'd watched headstrong horses. "I been thinking you ought to sell him now. No use waiting anymore." He paused again. "I talked to that fellow I know, runs Safariland up the other side of New Braunfels. Offered us a good price, enough to send someone to school."

I remained silently squatting down. My life had grown so complicated that Bengal didn't seem to remember me, the simple boy who'd once wrestled him. He just lay on his tattered sling chair accepting a petting from someone familiar.

"Not yet," I said, pressing farther through the bars. "Don't sell him quite yet."

"All right," Dad said. "I guess I know how you feel."

Chapter
13

Aᴜᴛᴜᴍɴ ᴡᴇɴᴛ ʜᴀʀᴅ ғᴏʀ ᴍᴇ ʙᴀᴄᴋ ᴀᴛ ᴄᴏʟʟᴇɢᴇ. The scrimmage had been an important event; Coach Grimes was deaf to my complicated excuses. At practices I became the team's second-favorite tackling dummy. According to NCAA rules, the coaches couldn't take my scholarship away, so they tried to make football so unpleasant that I'd quit. Unfortunately I'm persistent, which meant great pain to the arms and legs.

I just thanked God I wasn't Randy, the team's favorite tackling dummy. He'd only played three minutes of the scrimmage — sufficient time to turn tail and run. The two long passes he'd miraculously snagged were completely forgotten when he'd handed the balls back to the charging linebackers.

"You should have fallen on it," I told him one evening as we walked. "Or run out of bounds or something."

"Shit, don't I know it, but I couldn't think. Those varsity buffaloes wanted the ball, so I gave it to them. And now Dad's written me out of the will, and my brother won't talk to me. I wasn't even invited home for Thanksgiving."

"Well I was," I said, sadly, "but I couldn't go. If I showed up, Rose wouldn't — and I wanted her to get at least one good meal. Claudine cooked roast goose, too, Bohemian-style."

My mouth watered in a melancholy way. Randy and I walked on, our lives in a mess. Down below the dorm a janitor was burning autumn leaves; it seemed the proper season for morbid nostalgia. And we were on our way to the evening's punishment session with the team trainer. His name was Cantina, and the evening sessions — reserved for Certified Team Shitheads — were called Cantina's Cantinas. We climbed the long stadium ramp to the training room very slowly, stopping at the slots to gaze out at the empty parking lots. The autumn breeze felt cool, especially on our bald heads. The varsity had shaved them as an additional torment.

"Remember high school ball?" Randy said.

"Do I?" We both leaned out the ramp slot to spit.

"And Coach House? I felt real bad about making him swallow his whistle."

"I know you did," I said. We shoved off and headed for the training room door.

Randy's posture was particularly sad; he hadn't been faring too well, even with the sorority girls. The only ones that would go out with bald boys were the Delta Zetas — otherwise known as the DZ's, or the Diseases. Randy sagged to a stop at the training room door.

"I almost envy Johnny Boni. My mother wrote he was

in a carload of soldiers that hit a bridge abutment. They buried him in a flag, at least."

"Come on, buddy." I opened the door. "Let's go forget ourselves in the joy of vigorous exercise."

Mr. Cantina did not look like the Marquis de Sade, except that his mustache resembled a French sneer. His training sessions were the simplest form of torture. Rather than kick or slap us around like Coach Grimes, he let us hurt ourselves, while he sat on his desk beside a photograph of his plump wife and three soft-looking daughters. Behind him on the wall hung the same poster I'd had in my attic bedroom — of a man without skin, with arrows naming the various muscles. It was a slim comfort to identify the muscle that was killing you.

The first fifteen minutes we warmed up with jumping jacks, with two twenty-five-pound dumbbells and the fifty-pound weight vest we wore all evening. Every count we missed added ten pushups to our final tally. No matter how strong you were, the exercises exceeded that limit. Next we did situps with our dumbbells, followed by pullups in the weight vest. Then running in place shouldering a hundred-pound barbell. Situps. Duck walking with barbell. Pullups. Run in place. Pushups. Neck bows. Duck walk. Squat thrusts. Situps. Neck bows. Duck walk. Squat thrusts. Run in place. We were also supposed to holler, but mostly we just squeaked.

The worst of all came last, naturally. Fifteen trips running up the stadium steps. It was a very tall stadium, and the pain drove you inside of yourself. Nightmarish hallucinations came in regular flashes. Swooning in pain I sometimes thought I was running upwards into the sky. It seemed the ascension after my death. I thought constantly of collapsing with fatal heart failure, and of Rose's presence at my simple funeral. I suppose these visions were building a warehouse full of good character.

Then, afterwards, Randy and I and the other Team Shitheads helped each other back to the dorm. Midway we stopped to rest at the bridge of a small bubbling brook. I've heard that wounded animals also run to water. The bridge was called Quitter's Leap, after the few fellows who'd jumped. We were all leaning over the rail listening to our sweat *plink* into the water.

"Hey," said a boy named Toll, "what's this collich like? You freshmen been to any classes?"

"A couple," I said. "Haven't you?"

Toll was a junior; he had little ability as a wide receiver, and to run him off the coaches had permanently assigned him to Cantina's Cantinas. But Toll still wouldn't quit. He came from West Texas.

"Oh, yeah," he said, "I went to a few my first year, out of curiosity, I guess. But hell, the team tutors give you all the quizzes. I couldn't see wasting my time."

Randy, who'd been staring over the bridge rail, said, "You know, if you're injured they can't take your scholarship away."

"Hmm," somebody said thoughtfully.

Randy leaned out a little farther. "How far down is it, you think?"

"Twenty feet," I said. "You might break an ankle, that's all. You'd be back on the squad in a week."

The coaches were notorious for making people with small broken bones play ball.

"Unless you broke your neck," said Toll, "but then you'd be one of them poor paralytics, that can't even masturbate."

For a while we all leaned farther over and considered this as an alternate future. It was Friday night, but for bald boys there seemed little else to do. Finally Toll rocked back and said:

"Shit a brick, but I want a gal. I'm goin' to get a house piece of ass, if any of you numb nuts want to come."

Randy pepped up a little. "Which sorority?"

Toll laughed. "I ain't talking about collich gals, you snoot. Ain't you ever been to a whorehouse?"

Randy hitched up his sweat pants. "I haven't had to."

"Well I have and I admit it. You go on up to your room with a magazine. Me, I'm goin' to the Chicken Ranch."

Randy thought about it just a moment, scratching where his curls used to be. "I'll drive."

I went back with them as far as the dorm lobby, and while they ran upstairs to change clothes, I went to my mailbox. Inside was a packet of letters Rose had sent back, unopened again. She was serious about not wanting to involve me in her life. Standing there in the lobby with a handful of unread, tender words made me feel mortally sad. The sound of grunting football players echoed down the staircase; my friends were going to the whorehouse. I went to the phone booth and called Rose's home. Shirley answered.

"You promised not to call."

"I know I did. But won't she even read my letters?"

Shirley paused. "Do you really expect her to? She hardly even speaks to me, and *I'm* right here."

"Well, put her on. I'll just read a few over the phone."

"I would," Shirley said, "but for your information she's not here. She's . . . she's out on another date."

Gurgling sounds came up my throat. "A date? She can't, she's pregnant! It's not safe!"

"Sure it is," Shirley said, twisting the dagger. "She doesn't even wear a diaphragm anymore. And there's nothing you can do about it, way up in Austin." *Click!*

I was silently waiting for the others in Randy's backseat, and I remained silent most of the way. Other lovers have experienced similar chest cramps. I thought about Rose's body — I didn't want anyone else sharing its plenty. But there seemed little I could do to stop it; Rose was a headstrong woman of late. So I sat in the backseat feeling so jealous I could have bitten myself.

The Chicken Ranch lies off Highway 71, midway between Austin and Merry. The moon was shining full that night, bathing the pastureland. This was hilly country — mountainous compared to my rice prairies — and nothing, not the tilting pastures or even the fenceposts, seemed to run straight up and down. At the Texaco station in La Grange, Toll bought a party pack of French ticklers, and distributed them after taking his choice. It was a shag of hair with a walrus's face. For sentimental and revengeful reasons, I took a redheaded tickler, made to look like Bozo the Clown.

Off the highway the whorehouse road curved, two-wheel paths and a spine of worn-down weeds, through a screen of live oaks into a farmyard full of pickups and young men's shiny cars. The house lay at the far end — an old, modified farmhouse of ordinary white clapboards, fronting the stump of an old shade tree. The front porch had been removed, to discourage rowdy serenades, I thought.

As we got out Randy started stuffing his keys in his front pocket, so his trousers looked filled out. Toll fell back on the car hood, hooting like a West Texas boy.

"What the Sam Hell you doing — they're gonna find out what you got soon enough. Just put them keys under the mat — if you lose them in there, it costs double to get them back."

A huge Negress, larger than two Texas Rangers, let us in and showed us down a dim plaster hall to the waiting room. Lagging behind I pretended to inspect framed prints of Lincoln and Kennedy, but in the reflection I pressed my lame ear flat. When I got nervous like this it tended to flap. When I looked up the Negress was watching me, fingering something blunt in her pocket.

The waiting room was crowded but there were no whores. I found a seat and sat down quickly, hoping to blend in. But really I wasn't kinky enough. The man beside me wore a Scottish tam o'shanter and a kilt. The three fellows on my left wore Stetsons with sheriff badges pinned to the brims. Across the room a man with skinny ankles held a newspaper over his face, hiding from someone in the room, and over nearer the Styrofoam ice chest (labeled BEER. PREMIUM. LOCAL) sat a mature man and woman. They looked very much alike — long narrow heads and pale complexions — and they had the aloof air of people experienced in a major depravity. It was a strange atmosphere, hard to describe, but when the whores came in I'd found a comparison that settled my mind.

It was the Miss Smith Dance School Cotillion. In the ladies swished, wearing the cheap bright dresses of the poorer Cotillion girls. Ladies' Choice. They split among the crowd, nudging each other in different directions. The deputies went first, of course. Then a chubby-breasted woman passed me for an Aggie in overalls. A sharp-breasted woman led Toll from the room, laughing at his walrus tickler. A cheekboned older gal with aggressive jewelry rubbed Randy's bald head, saying, "You look just like Elvis, when he went in the Army."

Would a prostitute ever rub my bald head, I wondered, or was I doomed to a life alone? Finally a woman sank down in the seat beside me. I was afraid to look at her directly, but she seemed old. She was massaging her neck with both hands.

"Do you ex-perience any difficulties with arousal?" She pronounced each syllable separately, like a poor reader.

"Not normally. Why, do you have to fill out a card for future reference?"

She smiled at this and introduced herself. "I'm Cinda, and I don't want no trouble."

"And I'm Balloons," I said. This made her look at me again, sizing me up.

"That right? You're Balloons, and you want me to blow you up?"

"No," I said, smiling nervously, "that's just my cover name. I don't want you blackmailing me when I'm famous."

She rolled her eyes and laughed. "Another weirdo. Follow me."

Overall, Cinda did not resemble a successful prostitute. She was pretty enough, with hair the color of raw pine, and her turquoise party dress scooped low in the back to a big cushioned bow, which rode the nice swell of her buttocks. But there was something exhausted about the way she walked, like a day person walking through a night person's job. The huge Negress noticed it, too, as we passed her in the hall. First she gave me a chilly, warning scan, then said to Cinda:

"Girl, you're dragging. Eat you a Snickers like I tole you. Might get you some energy."

Cinda just groaned and marched on, with me following a discreet distance behind. Why I wanted to be discreet in a whorehouse, I don't know.

Cinda's room — a bed with a slick spread, a dresser, and a mirror dusty with talc — surprised me because I hadn't thought she lived here, too. Under the bed I might find a stuffed giraffe, a stack of warped records, a shoebox full of old ribbons and ticket stubs.

Cinda, however, felt less sentimental about her room. She washed her hands methodically at the sink and dried them with a rough, manilla-colored towel.

I thought I ought to make some conversation. "Is the food good here?"

No answer. All business. She minced toward me to close the door I'd forgotten.

183

"It's twelve dollars regular, eighteen-fifty oral, forty-five —"

"Regular! I'm regular. Strictly regular," I said. But I wondered what cost forty-five dollars.

"Yeah," she said, as if confirming meager expectations. She sat down on a short stool by the sink. "Com'ere and take your pants down." She pronounced it "pa-ints."

"Why? I'm regular."

"Ex-amination time. I got to check your thang for nasty business. You know, pus, crabs, dis-charges —"

"Okay!"

With my Fruit of the Looms lowered I explained that it wasn't likely I carried any nasty business; I'd been a good boy all my life. She began probing anyway. Her head moved in curious, inspective circles. As a kid at the Herman Park Zoo in Houston, I'd spent hours watching the spider monkeys. Off in the corner, I remembered, two of them had squatted like this, inspecting each other for lice. And here we are, I thought, two curious monkeys. I touched Cinda's raw pine hair.

She slapped my hand away. "What the shit you doing, messing my hi-air?"

"No, you know — I was just thinking. Have you ever watched monkeys?"

She raised her eyes; her eyebrows came up, starting a little wave of wrinkles. She smiled, or grinned, then thought better of it, snapping my waistband closed.

"There's no monkey business here. You want that kind of fun, go down to Laredo."

I nodded. I was definitely in the wrong place, but there

seemed no getting out of it now. Cinda was busy washing her hands again.

"Okay, now you can check me. Ordinary I can't gar-antee anything, but we just had our medical so you can bet I'm clean. Of a usual we do it on Thursday but 'cause the road crew was doing the highway, she wanted to wait till they brung in ever-thing they had. Anyway, it's your turn."

"No, thanks. I'll take your word." What would I check for anyway?

She took my money and left the room. I heard her down the hall talking to the Negress, who was telling her to watch me.

"Doan you play none of your napping tricks on that boy. Could be a mean one, the look of his ear."

Feeling self-conscious I went to the mirror to straighten my ear, and fiddling with it I knocked something over on the dresser. It was an ant farm — a clear plastic box filled with yard dirt and house ants. The top had popped off, spilling half of them out. Some ran back and forth, seeming to count survivors, while others reared up to wipe off their antennas. I swept as many as I could back inside, but then — hearing footsteps in the hall — I brushed the survivors onto the carpet and stamped them into the fiber. When Cinda came in I was wiping my hands on my jeans and looking very guilty. Fortunately she was in a hurry and didn't notice.

"Thought you'd be ready for me," she said coldly, and went right to work getting undressed. She knew exactly where her dress zipper was, under the cushioned bow, and the dress was still swinging on its nail in the wall when she spread out on the bed. Against it, her buttocks and thighs flattened out, like something soft thrown against something hard.

"You better hop on quick, Mister Baboons. You didn't pay all night."

I lay down beside her, nervously naked. I thought I ought to pay her one compliment, at least.

"You have great lips," I said.

She didn't immediately know what to think of that, and glanced at my face to see what kind of fool I was. Then she glanced at my naked parts, which were showing no evidence of being in the mood.

Cinda smiled slightly. "Hooray! I knew I'd guessed right again. You're one of them boys who just wants to talk."

Since she didn't seem terribly disappointed, I wasn't either. In fact, I felt suddenly more friendly with Cinda. She was obviously the whorehouse goof-off.

"Yeah, let's talk. Tell me about your pet ants."

"Oh, no," she said, visibly relaxing and looking fondly across the room at her little stinging friends. "I could talk about them little devils all night, and you didn't pay that long. Besides, you're supposed to do the talking — I get to lay here with my eyes closed. I'll be listening, I promise, but I need to close my eyes to concentrate."

She closed her eyes and before I finished two sentences she began to snore. When I was certain she was completely asleep, I confessed to her that I'd stomped on some of her pets. After that I couldn't think of a thing to say — at least to her. It was another woman, *my* woman, who I needed to talk to.

I got up quietly and dressed quickly, so quickly that I forgot some of my clothes. In the next room a noisy fellow was taking his post-sex French bath in the sink, but his splashing didn't wake Cinda either. On my way out I stopped long enough to pick a few crippled survivors out of the carpet fiber and return them to the shaken ant farm.

At the door to the parking lot I ran into the huge Negress again. She acted friendlier now, but seemed suspicious that I'd finished so fast.

"She fall asleep on you?"

"No, no," I lied. "Cinda was a pillar of prostitution; she gave me everything I needed and more."

I guess I laid it on a little thick, because I liked Cinda. The big Negress studied me a moment, then laughed. In a way she resembled the older ladies in town who had adopted me, though they probably would have resented the comparison. In addition, she had a beautiful deep laugh. I was looking out the door to make sure the Bonneville was still empty, while handing her every dollar in my wallet.

"What you giving me this for?"

"My friends, those other bald-headed boys," I said. "I've got to borrow the car, but I want them to have a good night."

I was already out the door but came back.

"Maybe I better tell you where I'm going, in case they ask."

The big Negress laughed again. "Oh, I already knows

that. We gets one boy like you a night — runs off to see the woman he came here to forget."

She paused to give me a friendly look, before going off to wake up Cinda. "But if this woman's new boyfrien' whup up on you, you come back. I doan like Cinda getting paid just to take a nap."

Chapter

14

Unfortunately I hadn't considered gas money, and ran out thirty miles from Merry. An hour's wait in the stinging sand whipped up by Interstate traffic. Finally a good-natured truck farmer with a load of Pecos cantaloupes picked me up and dropped me at Rose's dirt driveway. He was a jolly, round-cheeked fellow who talked in an easy way about the hard times of a cantaloupe farmer, what with nematodes plaguing his acres, and when I jumped down I wished him good luck with the truck scales (he was overweight) and good speed.

"Hell," he said, grinding first gear, "I'll be moving with the speed of a cantaloupe."

Then I was alone in the front yard under the high, autumn prairie moon. It shone through the bare limbs of the big pecan with a sort of desolation that made my jealous atoms ache. Lonely geese honked from out in the rice stubble.

First I crept around in the forsythias, window-peeping so my ears didn't show. Shirley was alone in the house, doing psychology homework by the light of the ten o'clock news. Because I was afraid of her I waited shivering under the big pecan. I wore only a T-shirt on top, having left my dress shirt back in Cinda's room. These miserable thoughts were in my mind: When would Rose come home, and how would I revenge myself on her date? Was *he* the other possible father-to-be, or were there others? How *many* others? The jealous moon seemed to penetrate my bones.

What was I, I thought under the cold bare limbs, was I one of Rose's jealousy-crazed operatic lovers trapped in a terrible plot? The answer seemed to be yes.

Gradually an ugly, operatic plot came to mind. Rose and her date might park right under this tree.

At about ten-thirty a Volkswagen Rabbit pulled into place. Laughter was heard inside. Then it grew quiet. Unable to restrain myself I dropped off the limb above, hollering like an opera tenor caught in barbed wire.

The two faces inside were shocked. They both sat up so fast their heads bumped the ceiling. Then Rose jumped out and threw her purse at me. The man with Rose was a woman.

"Bubber! You could have made us miscarry!"

"I'm sorry." I picked up her purse but held it behind me. Rose had a purse-hitting look in her eye.

Her friend got out saying, "This is Bubber?" She had a vaguely familiar face and a sense of humor. "You said he was wild, but you didn't tell me he swung from trees. Hello, I'm Nancy Walker."

She was very pregnant, even more so than Rose's six months. We shook hands over her baby.

"Yes, ma'am, I remember you. Dr. Frank almost sewed

your hand to my leg. I'm real sorry — I hope you're not hemorrhaging or anything. Shouldn't you check?"

"Oh, I'd know," she laughed. "But you make Rose calm down. She's been cranky and sarcastic for weeks — ever since she had to quit running." She got back in the Rabbit very carefully. "Rose — next class?"

"I'll drive. By then you won't fit under the steering wheel."

Nancy laughed and drove off. I walked Rose to the porch, giving back her purse as a gesture of peace. Since she didn't want to talk, I kept up a steady stream.

"Be careful. Watch that step. Up we go. Now give me the keys; I'll get the door. What class? Are you a coed?"

"I *wish*." Fumbling she found the keys herself but didn't open the door. She didn't want me inside. She settled back on one foot to outwait me.

"Then what sort of class is it?"

"Lamaze — natural childbirth. What are you doing here?"

"We're having our fetus naturally?" For some reason I felt overjoyed. "Oh, boy!"

"*You're* not having anything. And *what* are you doing here?"

"You're mad. Be careful, the fetus can feel it." I laid my hand toward her stomach but she brushed it away.

"What *are* you doing here?"

I lowered my head ashamed. "Shirley told me you were out on a date. It's a long story but I lost my head."

"You've lost something else. What happened to your hair?"

Before I could answer Shirley opened the door, her

thumb in a book. She took one look — "Oh, God, it's *him* again!" — and slammed the door. Then she reopened it.

"You're bald —"

"— as a baby," I said.

Rose snorted and pushed her way inside. She certainly knew how to make a path with her stomach. I followed, with Shirley in my wake.

"Rose, honey, listen —"

"He called you honey, Momma. This is distorting my whole adolescence."

"Go to your room, Shirley."

"Rose, please, tell me what's happening to our fetus. Does she have a face yet?"

"Ugh! My teen years are ruined."

"Go to your room, Shirley," I snapped.

"Harumpf!"

I turned back to Rose. "Please, share the fetus with me."

Adamantly silent, she had stretched out on the sofa, her stomach rising dramatically. Something was reprogenating in there, something important to me.

"This isn't fair. You can't keep this to yourself. At least tell me about these classes."

"*I*'ll tell you." Shirley wouldn't be left out. "She and that other divorcée are planning to help each other deliver. It's insane."

"No, it's not." Rose sat up, awkwardly clutching the sofa back. "With any luck this baby will turn out better than you."

"With Dumbo here for a father? I doubt it."

192

I cleared my throat. "I may not be the father. Rose says she was fooling around."

"Oh *sure* — you don't know Momma like me."

"Both of you be quiet! You're making my baby squirm."

Shirley and I shut up instantly and took a few automatic steps toward her. Rose's stomach seemed awesome, a monument. Shirley spoke first.

"Hot chocolate, Momma?"

"I'd rather have tea."

"No," Shirley said firmly. "Think of the caffeine."

Rose sighed.

"And, here, honey, I'll put a pillow under your feet."

"No, you go help Shirley. I want to be alone."

The kitchen smelled of carrot cake. Shirley put on a little plaid apron with "Big Mama" stitched across the bosoms. I stood idly by as she heated the milk. She seemed to resent my presence, but only mildly.

"Out of my way, Goofus." She opened the oven and took out a fresh carrot cake, her mother's favorite.

"Shirley, why'd you lie on the phone tonight? You knew your mother wasn't out on a date. You just wanted to get me here, didn't you?"

Shirley looked up. "Did I?" I couldn't tell what she was thinking, but there were devious schemes in her brain.

"I think you did — and I'm willing to call a truce. The situation calls for it, don't you think? How's she doing, really?"

There was enough concern in my voice that Shirley

glanced at me, the absentee father. "How does *any* thirty-five-year-old unwed mother who doesn't want to admit her condition act? You tell me, Mr. Smarts."

I nodded, then hung my head. "Cranky and sarcastic."

"The only time she's bearable is when Uncle Ben calls."

"Is there anything I can do?"

Shirley glanced at me again. In some way, and just somewhat, she had changed. She had a softer edge to her face; maybe taking care of her mother had mellowed her. Her hair was cut shorter, too. She went about slicing the first wedge off the cake, a wedge huge enough for two people.

"All right, quit looking snake-bit. I'll let you carry this tray in. But don't eat any cake yourself. Momma needs twice her calories now."

I saw what she meant. There were two lives now when we spoke of Rose. I took the tray very thankfully.

"But don't get any ideas," Shirley cautioned me. "This is a truce, not a surrender. I just have to go to the bathroom and I don't want the chocolate getting cold."

I gave her my most direct look. "And *I* don't want to play tug of war with the fetus. A truce?"

She stopped at the door and considered me with a good long look. I assumed she was thinking about my character, my ability to carry fatherhood, but she wasn't. "You know," she said, "with your head shaved, Big-ears, you look like a taxi cab with both doors open."

Rose was laughing softly at this when I came in. "I see you two still get along. But really, you do look awful." There was a familiar tender look in her eyes when she made fun of me; it warmed my heart.

"Hot." I handed her the cup. "Careful. Are you-all feeling better now?"

"Fine." She sipped. "Just exhausted."

"Maybe you two shouldn't rest on the sofa. I didn't mend it too well."

She smiled, remembering the day I'd moved in. "Oh, I reglued it after you left for work."

We sat awhile, listening to Shirley pee down the hall. We hadn't heard her doing that the morning she'd moved out; we probably should have guessed her surprise.

"Do you still stink?" I asked, taking her free hand.

"Yes." She patted it. "More than ever. But before you sniff me, hand me the cake."

She couldn't quite reach it over her stomach, which rose magnificently under her rainbow-striped muslin blouse. Maybe she didn't show as much as I imagined; probably she looked like any woman who'd devoured a tub of carrot cake with her fingers. But she did hold a fetus inside; I kept imagining its feelings in the womb. It must be like living inside a tent.

Rose stopped chewing and made a face. Something was happening inside.

"Can I — can I?" I stammered a little with emotion.

Rose knew what I meant. Shirley came back right then — "You forgot the fork" — and saw what we were doing. She hesitated at the door a moment; her mother looked happier now, with me here.

"Can I touch, too?"

Rose looked up. "Sure, you both can — together. After all, neither of you could have managed alone."

Both fathers-to-be were kneeling with our hands on her

stomach when we felt the first fetal kick. Physically, it could be compared to a sleepy Cub Scout in a pup tent. Emotionally it was more sublime. Somehow or other, through the most unconventional means, the three of us had managed to spawn life. Rose finished her carrot cake watching us, the two people she loved who were wrecking her life.

That night I slept on the floor beside Shirley's bed; Rose had moved there to be nearer the bathroom because her bladder was smaller now. She stepped on me several times getting up to go, but I didn't so much as yelp. Early the next morning Shirley drove me with a gas can to the Bonneville. We talked along the way, and I told her I was going to take Lamaze classes, too.

"She said I could be part of it."

"Not without me, you're not. We'll start when I get there in January."

"You're coming to college? I thought the money —"

Shirley made a noise that sounded remarkably like a laugh. Was she learning how?

"Daddy finally got what he deserved. His disability checks came to his old address, and Momma cashed them all last week. You know, it's strange. I get to go to college because my mother forged the checks that my father deserved because his mistress shot him in the leg. That bitch La Vonne — I ought to write her a thank-you note." She paused reflectively. "So, you can't start classes without me."

"But look, Shirley, you've got to face facts. You're not as much a part of this as me."

"Don't," she cautioned, "play tug-of-war with the fetus."

"Then listen — you're going to be left out sooner or later. It's just a matter of time before she breaks down and marries me."

Shirley let out a peal of excellent laughter; maybe driving my De Soto had given her a sense of humor.

"She never will. She's got too much pride to marry you."

"And what's wrong with me?"

"Besides the obvious, you're fifteen years younger."

"Fourteen and a half — and she can outrun me."

"People on the street don't know that."

Shirley had a point, but I ignored it.

"What else?"

"No education — face it, Bubber, you've got no job future. Why *would* she marry you?"

I thought a moment, then said, "Love."

"Weird — it'll never work."

"Well," I said, "we'll see."

Chapter
15

I SET OUT TO PROVE TO SHIRLEY (AND TO MYSELF) that I wouldn't be a misfit as a husband. I started getting up early, combing my hair with cold water, and studying each morning through noon into night. I needed to study, since I was failing college. Most of the ballplayers used the team's crooked tutoring facilities and received exemplary grades, but dishonesty seemed a poor way to prove myself as a family man.

But getting tackled to the edge of consciousness every afternoon took its toll. Regular season play was almost over, and the boys who'd used my body as a dummy had grown tremendously in their ability to crush me. One rainy afternoon I simply didn't show up at practice — I went to the quiet library instead — and the next day I explained that my grandmother had died. By mid-December I'd killed off eight or nine grandparents, and Coach Grimes had become suspicious. He called me into his office.

"HOW MANY YOU GOT ANYWAY?" He shouted so the other boys could hear. He'd closed the venetian blinds that looked out on the locker room, but they could easily eavesdrop over the short office walls. I was going to be made an example of.

"We're a very large family," I explained quickly, "but there's never been any inbreeding."

Coach licked his lips, as though preparing to bite into a liar. I automatically crossed myself like a Catholic. This caught Coach's attention. He hadn't known I was religious. A sort of inner calm rose up in the reborn Christian. Perhaps there was a more Christlike way of dealing with me. He asked me to sit down, then pulled a huge family Bible from his desk drawer. There was something touching about an overweight forehead gazing sacredly down at the Bible. Its tattered pages seemed to move him. He spoke in the softest voice I'd heard him use.

"My own grandma," he said, "ran back into two burning houses for this Book. Why do you want to lie about yours? She's not dead, is she? Just tell me where you been, son, out with the girls?"

I was moved to speak the truth. "No, sir. At the library, sir."

Coach reacted with complete disbelief. What kind of ballplayer went to libraries? I hurried to explain.

"I'm trying to get my grades up, so I can transfer to A and M. I think I'm going to be a vet."

Saying this was a mistake, too. Texas A&M was the university's major gridiron rival; just two years ago the Aggies had kidnapped our team mascot, Bevo the Longhorn bull, and barbecued him. Outside in the locker room the boys quieted down so they could hear Coach kill me. But stunned, he had instinctively put his hand over the

Good Book, so as to prevent it from witnessing my blasphemy. Before he could rise up and smite me, I spoke.

"I think I'd better quit the team. Why don't you give my scholarship to someone else."

Since that was what Coach wanted, he relaxed. He allowed that sometimes quitters do the team a lot of good, but he'd sure miss using me as a tackling dummy.

"Cotton Bowl's coming up," he said, ushering me out, "and all we got left is that buddy of yours — the one that screams when they stick him." He shook his head. "I don't know, I just don't know, you'd think folks in Texas could raise better boys."

My first final exam was held later that week in a vast, remotely lit auditorium in the new government building. The lighting was modern, and I sat among nearly a thousand other purple-faced Gov. 101 students answering the essay question, "What makes America tick?" At the end of two hours we all got up, light-headed from having thought so hard, and bumped into each other trying to escape out the door. Outside, the sudden sunlight bewildered us and I bumped into many blinking students on my way across Quitter's Leap. I was on a journey to clean out my locker.

In the locker room I stood a moment, listening to the distant thuds of practice in session. Football had been good for me; the running around grunting, the jumping on other boys, the pushing and plunging until the last whistle had blown; and I'd miss the excitement and the glory and the simple pleasure of a clean cross-body block. And especially, I'd miss my uniform. I'd sweated so much into that thing that it almost had a life of its own. But I couldn't have football, college, a wife, and a child.

I pushed my equipment through the laundry room chute and was digging several fossilized jockstraps out of my locker, when two varsity no-necks dragged Randy's body in. They deposited it scornfully on a bench, where it clutched its knee and squinted until the no-necks ran back out.

"Bubber, am I glad it's you. Help me over the Health Center fast — I heard the cartilage snap."

I carried him out to the car and on the drive over asked if he was in much pain. He was singing a Christmas carol, "Deck the Halls," through clenched but grinning teeth.

"It's terrible. Ex*cru*ciating. I'll never play ball again." Then he went back to singing: " 'Tis the season to be jolly, fa la la, la la la."

But at the Health Center wheelchair ramp, the pain took his breath away. I was shouldering him up the incline.

"You don't think I'll be crippled for life?"

"No," I said. "But what's a slight limp on an educated man? Just be thankful you're alive."

"Yeah." He brightened and sneered, as if he'd just thought of something. "That's right. I get to keep my scholarship." As if he'd just thought of it.

I shuffled a few steps farther, Randy in my arms. Though he appreciated all my help, he didn't like being this close to another male animal. "I'm gonna need someone better to lean on, someone with money and tits. Maybe I'll call that senator's daughter in Poli Sci; she keeps looking at me like I've got a political future."

While his cast dried in the Health Center corridor, Randy made a wheelchair call to this girl, and arrangements were made to meet at Schultz's Beer Garden. Belinda would drop by after dinner, which she was having nearby at the governor's mansion. I was asked along, too, mainly as Randy's crutch; the Health Center had run out of them during regular season play.

On the way over that evening Randy gave me explicit instructions; he laid siege on women like a general or a quarterback, and he planned to use his injury to advantage. I was not to talk politics, I was not to mention my love life, I was not to speak at all. After ten minutes, I should jump up, mumble that I'd forgotten I had an exam in the morning, and run off to leave them alone. Belinda, it seemed, lived in a garden apartment near Barton Springs, and Randy planned for her to take him there, where she'd nurse his wounds by taking off all her clothes.

Schultz's was packed that night, with students living like there was no exam tomorrow. The jukebox could barely be heard spilling out Bing Crosby Christmas carols, but the crowd had inhaled too much red and green beer to be attentive. Still, the call of the Yuletide season was present, and one fraternity drunk had come wearing a Santa costume. He only let girls sit in his lap, whispering in their ears, "Pretend I'm not wearing trousers."

"If he does that to Belinda," Randy said, "I want you to knock out his stuffing."

"Certainly," I said. "I'd be happy to. But won't beating up Santa Claus depress your date?"

Randy hunkered farther over his red beer and shot me a worried glance. "That's *just* the kind of wisecrack I don't want. Come on, buddy, put on your best behavior — this is more than an ordinary piece of ass."

"I can see that," I said, watching Belinda enter the beer garden. Schultz's, near the capitol building, was a lunchtime haunt for the politicians, and Belinda seemed to know her way around. She was a leggy but ugly-above-the-neck Texas gal, from an outspoken, ambitious household. Senator Buchanan, Randy later told me, owned many several-thousand-acre ranches, where the grazing cattle all tripped over the oil wells. So far the senator had been the district attorney, the congressman, and the governor, and now he wanted to be something else. Belinda had his way of canvassing the crowd, spotting us and taking note of everyone else. On her way over she shrewdly skirted the horny Santa and sat down. Randy had hobbled up to pull out her chair.

"Well, aren't you nice?" she said. She was big-boned and wore her nice clothes poorly, like a rancher in a crushed-velvet dress. "But sit down. How's your leg?"

"Fine," Randy said, as if barely bearing up.

"Will it really take you off first-string?"

Randy avoided my eyes. "I'm afraid so. But I'm thinking of using my spare time like you suggested."

"Student politics? That's a good idea, Randy — Daddy started that way himself."

"I didn't know that," Randy said, taking her hand. His charm was oozing all over Belinda. "You'll have to tell me all about his rise to fame."

Belinda smiled. She had respectable bosoms, but they were dominated by her square, Texas politician's jaw. Randy overlooked this flaw because she was rich and powerful. She was also political enough to notice my presence.

"Randy, why don't you introduce your friend?"

"I'm sorry," I said, reaching across the table to shake her hand. "I'm Bubber Drumm, Randy's crutch for the evening, and I'm not supposed to talk."

Randy nudged me under the table. It was already time to go. But just to tease him I decided to stay. My dorm room was lonely, and Belinda seemed a nice girl, once you got used to looking at her. She had eyelashes like a cow's.

"Why shouldn't you talk?"

"Oh, Randy's afraid I'll mention my love life."

"His girlfriend won't marry him," Randy said. "It's an old story. Let's talk about my knee."

But Belinda was more polite than him. "Why won't she marry you — are you a Republican?"

I laughed. "No, I'm conservative but not that bad."

"Then why?" Belinda did seem interested. Her family had thrived on other people's scandals.

"Ha," Randy said, trying to turn off the limelight, "you name a problem, he's got it. She's the mother of his ex-girlfriend, for one thing. In our hometown he couldn't get elected dog-catcher."

But Belinda was too curious to stop probing now. First, she put Randy in his place. "You wanted to know the secret to Daddy's success? It's a quote he read in the Bible: 'Speak you the truth quietly and clearly; and listen to others, even the dull and the ignorant; they too have their story.'"

She turned back to me.

"It began in a small Texas town," I said, sitting back.

"And she's thirty-five," Randy interrupted, "and pregnant."

"Her daughter helped me do that."

"You or somebody else."

"Me, I'm pretty sure."

"Order me a daiquiri, Randy," Belinda said, "and quit interrupting." She encouraged me to go on. I began with the first conversation under the worm-dripping tree, then ran to being tasted, stitched, bombarded by books, kissed, and unhinged at the ear. Like most people, especially intelligent ones, Belinda enjoyed listening to stories. Randy didn't. Valuable sex time was being wasted. He fidgeted at first, then took aim and kicked me with his cast. Since I was almost finished anyway, I told the ending of the abortion clinic chapter while halfway under the table rubbing my shin.

"Wow," Belinda said, "and I thought politics was wild. You ought to write this down — it'd sell millions more than Lyndon's brother's book."

That book, a best-seller, had aired the filthy family laundry.

"Aw," Randy said, "millions?"

"Certainly," Belinda replied. "And I know what I'm talking about. Daddy polls me on every issue. He says I'm absolutely average."

Randy took her hand again. "I don't think you are."

I came up from under the table, slowly.

"Millions?"

Back at the dorm I sat down at my miniature desk and began to scribble some notes. With millions I might be able to support a family. But despite Belinda's enthusiasm

I couldn't seem to get it down on paper properly. I didn't want the public prying into every sex act, and the notes about true love seemed corny. About the time I felt thoroughly discouraged, my roommate Ruby came in from the showers and went to his desk. He hadn't learned to read yet, but his textbooks were neatly arranged by weight. He selected a heavy Webster's, and banging it tentatively on his brain, he came to look over my shoulder. My studying always intrigued him.

"Hey man, what's that?"

What did words on a page look like to him?

"It's writing. I'm trying to write a book."

"Oh." Ruby nodded. "Yeah." He knew what books were good for. "Try and make it a two-pounder. I need one about that size."

That weekend I moved out of the dorm, into a small dilapidated cabana nestled among other peeling cabanas, under the flight path of the Austin municipal airport. From my bed I could reach the refrigerator, and when I showered I also washed the dishes. But all things considered the Heart of Texas Cabanas were nice; they were originally intended to resemble paradise — with peach, banana, and papaya trees lining the common courtyard, which now had the air of fallen fruit. On the warm winter evenings I lounged outside on the crooked lawn furniture, cooking suppers on a home-built barbecue pit. It was made from a castoff porcelain sink and refrigerator grill, and many hours were spent reading and studying by the light of that fire. Naturally my neighbors thought me strange. They were all neatly attired men who held hands;

apparently they'd been driven out of the decent neighborhoods, too. So, on the whole my life was fine: contemplative, solitary, and inexpensive. I took up smoking a Dr. Graybow tobacco pipe and brooding deeply, two habits found in mature men.

Twice a week I called Rose for condition reports; she seemed to accept her pregnancy and my involvement now, even to appreciate some of it, but she remained adamant on the subject of marriage. We'd already paid the price of our dalliance, she thought.

The Heart of Texas phone was located in the courtyard under a speckled tin dishpan, beside a tricky aluminum lawnchair. One windy cold night, as a sleeting norther blew from the Panhandle down the neck of my jean jacket, I mentioned a book I was reading to Rose.

"I'm worried about pain. This fellow talks about it all the time."

"What fellow? What book is this?"

"*Painless Childbirth*, by Fernand Lamaze."

Rose laughed. "I'd better not tell Shirley you're reading ahead."

"No, don't! Please. But what about this pain?"

My voice was urgent; Rose laughed again. "You're going to be a big help, I see that. But don't worry. With Shirley I didn't need a spinal block. Your dad calls me an easy breeder."

"How *is* that old fencepost? He hasn't written me in months."

Rose didn't answer me for a moment. "He's not real well. It's nothing serious, just his age. Maybe you ought to stay with him over the holidays."

"But Claudine's there. And I want to be with you."

"Maybe," she said, "you ought to stay with him."

I wish I could say Dad's problem was the normal, extreme nostalgia of the Christmas season, but it wasn't — it was his mind. And it was Time, too, which we think of as a line that runs in front and in back of us. It seems that when the line in front of us gets shorter, the line in back becomes more important. In the evenings, when Claudine was off at her job, Dad sat in his huge reading chair digging his way through layers and layers of magazines, but often stopping, gazing at the blinking Christmas lights, forgetting exactly where he was located on the long line of his life. His mind seemed to churn and his memories tumble. The first cow he'd loved, a nasty roan colt he'd broke, the cool sand under the family ranch house, Abby's petticoats rustling when she climbed into his yellow buggy and a song they'd sung during some war with the words "I want a little Belgium baby," the two times everyone paid their bills and he was rich, and the way the wind blew in 1932, Claudine brushing her hair, Loops in his lap, his boy off at college, the spot of chipped bark where his dad had broken his neck.

Sometimes these multiple memories were pleasant, startlingly lucid, and in a way his mind had never seemed so sharp. Why, he could relive at random most of his life; it was like being born again, almost. Unfortunately, though, these memories could not always be confined to the armchair. The morning I came home for the holidays, for instance, he thought I was in third grade. He met me at the door on the way out, with his vet's satchel.

"Where your books, boy?"

At the time I didn't understand. "I don't need books. We finished the term."

"In April? You go wash up and tell that to your mama. I'm missing supper myself. McAllister's trying to cover all his cows in one evening; his bull's nearly spent."

Claudine, who'd been dusting snakequariums, took me by the arm before I could stop him. She led me down an aisle. "He'll be all right. Just let him figure it out."

Outside, Dad started looking around for his old vet truck, and when he couldn't find it, he looked up at the rising winter sun.

It wasn't April, durn it! Or evening either! Growling, he kicked the Goodyear display so hard that Bengal blinked in his sling chair. Then after a few angry circles he stomped back inside.

"I'm turning into a mindless fool, boy. You seen the evidence yourself."

Claudine went stoically back to her dusting. "We'll all be where you are, if we're not struck down too soon. Just don't you kick no more chairs; we're short for Christmas dinner already."

Slightly ashamed Dad dumped himself into his reading chair. After a moment of rubbing his tangled eyebrows though, he started chuckling.

"Old McAllister's brahma — he was so wore out it took six cowboys to lift him on the last cow."

Claudine chuckled along with him. "The spirit's willing but the flesh is weak. I guess we *both* know how that is."

Dad looked up, full of appreciation for Claudine. For a

Bohemian she was a pretty good woman. "The worst of it is, honey, now I'm hungry for supper. Do we have to wait all day?"

Claudine shook her head and grinned. "The clock's still the clock, Charlie. And it's only nine-thirty now."

Chapter

16

"DAD'S DYING," I SAID. "MAKE HIS LAST DAYS happy and marry me."

Rose, who swayed gently in the porch hammock, wiggled her bare feet in the Christmas Eve sun. She finished a spoonful of chocolate mint ice cream, shaking her head over me.

"You'd use anything, wouldn't you? But Charlie's not dying, not yet, and I'm not repeating mistakes."

"But mistakes make evolution possible," I said, holding out the tub of ice cream. "I learned that in Anthropology. And just remember: you've done everything else I've asked."

"Don't I know it." Rose patted her twenty-nine-pound stomach and dipped into the tub. Inside the house the phone rang, and Shirley's footsteps raced to answer it. Rose decided to change the subject.

"So, you're really going to transfer — pre-vet and all?"

"Next fall," I said, "when you, young Abby, and Bengal can travel. We'll all get a garage apartment in College Station and —"

"And you'll come home from class all covered with manure," Rose finished my thought. "Sounds romantic, but we may be long gone by then."

"To where?" I asked, but Shirley interrupted:

"Long distance. Uncle Ben and June again."

Rose collected herself and with an agile swing came out of the hammock on her feet. Every time she did that, my heart stopped. What did the fetus feel, in midair? Will we ever come down? Is this The End? Will I never know my dear father?

After Rose left, Shirley came out with a spoon and lay down. She seemed greatly at peace with herself, eating ice cream from the bucket.

"Nice of you to bring this," she said.

"Well, don't eat so much. You're liable to look pregnant and run off the boys."

Shirley ate a vindictive spoonful. "Men turn me off."

"But what about Tire-iron? You two used to enjoy the same things, like collecting ears."

"Oh," Shirley laughed, "I haven't seen Tyronne since he stole the mayor's Cadillac. They put him in jail for fifty years."

I felt an unexpected sadness for the fellow who'd loosened my ear. "That's terrible—fifty years? But there's a better class of guys up at college. You'll find someone there."

"I doubt it," she said, but gave me a sideways glance. "How's Ransom doing, anyway?"

"Now Shirley, I don't want my possible-stepdaughter-to-be messing around with him; a rabbit's got better morals. Besides, he's spending the holidays with the senator's family. They're out in California testing the political waters."

"California!" Shirley flounced, disappointed. "That's all I hear about anymore."

Christmas dinner might have gone well, except that Bengal ate his first. About one o'clock Claudine, Dad, Rose, Shirley, and I were setting the table in the front room, when Sinclair and Lucy Taylor arrived with the extra chairs and the wine punch. They'd been sampling it on the way, of course.

"That damned tiger," Sinclair said, watching me carry all the chairs in, "he took a swipe at the man that runs down his feed. Nearly made me spit out my teeth. Where you want this chair, Claudine — at the head of the table for Loops? Com'ere you ugly thing — take a load off your legs."

Sinclair scooped up a section of Loops, who'd been lounging under the table digesting rats, and plopped him into a chair. Loops hated to be moved suddenly after a meal. Within seconds they — Loops, the chair, and Sinclair — had become one coughing, flailing, gagging unit.

"Holp! Holp!" Sinclair hollered.

"Goll-durn it, Sinclair." Dad threw down his stack of forks. He'd been in bad humor all day. "This time I hope he eats you."

"I'll get him off, Dad. Shirley, give me a hand."

"You're *crazy*. I'm not touching that snake."

"I will," Rose said. "Charlie, move back. It's not good for you to bend down."

Dad stepped dizzily away. In a moment we'd taken off enough coils that Sinclair could breathe. "I'm glad he's only one piece," he squeaked. "With arms and legs this snake'd be dangerous."

At that moment Lucy Taylor distracted us by calling from the kitchen. "Claudine, does this icebox still work?"

"I think so."

"Well, the ice cubes is all melted."

"Great," Dad groaned, and flopped down in his reading chair. He surveyed the mess of his house. Claudine, his illegal Bohemian roommate, was on hands and knees cleaning Pierce and Magnolia's nest from under the Frigidaire; apparently the nest had clogged and burned out the motor. Meanwhile drunk Sinclair was wrestling with a chair and being crushed by a massive python, who the illegitimate-father-to-be and the redheaded unwed mother were trying to unknot. And nearby, Shirley tapped on the snakequarium of Henry the timber rattler, who struck and bounced his face off the glass. This was his old-fashioned Christmas dinner? The old vet put his head in his hands.

"What's the matter, Dad? Feel sick?"

"No," he said, "I'm trying to go senile. Now leave me alone."

"Oh quit grumping, Charlie. You've been in a chair-kicking mood too long." Claudine came down the connecting hall to help us unravel Loops. "And there's customers coming. Now go be nice to them; it's Christmas."

A glossy station wagon full of presents had pulled up to the pumps. A young husband with a suede sports coat and low-cut shoes jumped out and danced to the passenger's side. He helped his wife out, who held a tender-looking, big-nosed baby. Apparently its diapers were soiled, because the couple talked in low tones about the possibility of germs in the restrooms. Behind them a creamy yellow Pekingese hopped down and began looking for a place to leave his mess.

Both humans were shocked by the sight of Dad rushing toward them. His face turned dark now when he walked fast, and Claudine dragging a python to the door didn't reassure them at all. The woman held the baby a little firmer, while the man went to the rear bumper and smiled. He'd seen strange things before, he thought.

"No Lead, please. Fill it." He then noticed Bengal sniffing at his shoes through the bars, and stiffened.

"Nothing to worry about with him," Dad said, straining to be polite. "Bengal was born in St. Louis. Tame as your baby boy — he's got his daddy's nose, I see."

The man glanced toward his son self-consciously. Dad went on: "While you're waiting, care to tour the serpentarium? Over a hundred snakes inside, most of them vanishing species."

The woman shook her head immediately, while the man moved away from Bengal as if to look inside. But after a very brief inspection of Loops, he shook his head.

"No thanks, just gas. We're in a hurry."

"Charlie," Claudine called from the door. "Watch that dog."

The Pekingese sniffed at the tidy pile of feces in the corner of Bengal's cage. Bengal was watching him as he resumed his parade of the bars.

"Shoo! Get gone!" Dad hollered, getting irritated. He turned back to the man. "You ought to educate yourself about snakes, Mister. They're ugly but they're important. One boa constrictor could rid your house of rats."

"Of course." The man glanced to his wife.

"What's the matter?" Dad asked in an unfriendly way. He was losing his temper now. "Have you got something against reptiles?"

The woman climbed back inside the car and the man took out his wallet. "That's fine . . . Enough gas."

Dad kept his hand clamped on the nozzle. "But you said fill it."

The man gave up on Dad and snapped his fingers for the dog. "Come, Linstrom, come here, boy."

But Linstrom was busy lifting his leg on Bengal's feces. He had apparently been riding a long time and needed to pee badly, because he didn't move when Bengal swept past. He was still there, lifting his leg with an intense expression of relief, when Bengal made his next circuit. The temptation was too much for the tiger.

One swat flattened the dog, whose eyes rolled, then bulged. Holding him down, Bengal stuck his jaws through the bars and bit off the dog's head. The woman screamed. The man shouted. Claudine cursed. Dad jerked tbe nozzle out and pumped gas on his boots, and inside we all rushed to look out the front window. Then the women rushed away again.

"Damn," Sinclair whistled with morbid admiration. "That animal's dying fast, at least."

And I said nothing, my leg scar tingling.

Meanwhile, Bengal raked Linstrom through the bars and snapped off all four legs and his little tail, swallowing them quickly because he knew he was doing something wrong. By the time I scrambled outside he'd finished gulping the torso, too, and was trying to scoop the head through the bars. I bent down cautiously to pick it up by the whiskers, but Dad stepped up and kicked it inside the cage.

"Better let him finish. These folks don't want to drive home with what's left."

The young couple sat in their front seat rubbing each other vigorously. The man was doing most of the comforting, though. The woman stared down at her little big-nosed baby and made menacing sounds.

"You're going to sue that man, Phillip. You're going to sue him for every red cent he's got."

"We'll talk to Tom when we get home, dear." He patted her shoulder and looked out at Dad. "You'll hear from our lawyer, rest assured."

After they'd driven off Dad walked slowly over to the water hose. Bengal had finished Linstrom now and was licking up the pavement, purring like a chainsaw.

"Rest assured," Dad repeated, bending down to turn the water on. Straightening up, his face was purple and his tone black. "It's time to turn the tiger loose, and this ought to be a lesson to you, boy — you can't hold on to things too long. That's been the problem of your life: holding on."

Rose appeared at the door and looked down on me. From her expression, she agreed with Dad. Only Bengal seemed unperturbed. As Dad hosed his cage floor clean he frolicked openly in the spray — a simple, pleasure-loving animal. I admit that I envied him.

Chapter
17

WITH ITS OWN SLOW MOMENTUM, COLLEGE moved on. I went to classes; I suppose I learned; I went to sleep at night. But if the experience had any flavor, I'd lost my sense of taste. Of course I liked reading R. Waldo Emerson, but trigonometry? The French and Indian Wars? What *I* needed were more practical courses, something I could sink my hands into. And I longed for the green piles of manure, which would be mine at veterinary school. What a pleasure, spending my days fixing simple, injured brutes. All I had to do was finish this year out, then transfer to Texas A&M. Still, it seemed a very long winter.

My load was lightened though, by Lamaze classes. Shirley and I attended, and we didn't just investigate birth, but the entire woman's body. An important and mysterious anatomy, responsible for procreating the human race. I plunged into it with an open heart. There was much more to Rose than her ligaments: her contracting tissues, her bones that bent, her Latin-sounding tunnels and the elaborate labyrinth of her sex. Her great internal vaults, too, and most secret, the sacred chamber where children are grown — curled, gnomish, and suspended head-down. One child in particular. Mine, my daughter-growing-to-be. But *what* would she be? *Which* pieces of ourselves, I wondered, would pass on? My elbows? Rose's feet? My big ears? — I hoped they'd become extinct.

However, at the Lamaze classes Shirley and I never told the truth. She was listed on the class roster as pregnant. Our teacher, Dr. O'Keefe, became suspicious when she noticed Shirley wasn't overweight, so I built an artificial pregnancy contraption. Actually, it was just several throw-pillows sewn together with a belt. Week by week I was building Shirley up — until one night in the middle of late February. She refused to look eight and a half months pregnant.

"I'm *not* your Frankenstein," she said. "*You* wear it; you're taking on all the other symptoms anyway."

"Now, now," I said. "I got over my morning sickness last week. Please put it on; we've only got two more classes."

"But what if Lawrence sees me?"

We were in her cabana, three doors down from mine, in the company of Fred and Hank from next door. Fred, forty-one, was a bookkeeper, and Hank, twenty-seven, was a carpenter turned housewife. He sewed all of Shirley's maternity clothes, which she wore when there was no possibility of seeing Lawrence, her new beau.

"But Larry won't see you," I said. "Tell her, Hank."

"He won't! He won't!" Hank bounced on the bed. He always acted ridiculously excited, like the housewives on TV. Fred reached over and patted his mate's hand.

"Hank's right. The chances are highly unlikely." Fred was a dignified older homosexual, always very precise. "Coincidence is rare."

"Not in *my* life, it isn't." Shirley threw the pillows at me.

But in the end, the obligations of fatherhood forced her to go, wearing sunglasses. In the De Soto out front of the YWCA I made her strap the pillows on, but she didn't belt them tight enough. By the time we'd climbed the front steps, the contraption had slipped, and Shirley looked pregnant at the knees. She waddled grumpily inside the lobby, where I tried to straighten her up in a phone booth. This meant I had to unbutton the back of her dress to rebelt the pillows, with Shirley muttering about Lawrence catching us. But it wasn't his footsteps approaching; it was Dr. O'Keefe's.

"Mr. MacDrumm?" she said. (I'd registered under an alias.) "Is your wife having trouble?"

Shirley was grunting and grouching, bent over holding up her pregnancy and her sunglasses.

"No, no," I said. "No trouble. No miscarriages here."

Dr. O'Keefe had given us a terrifying lecture on those, and I never saw her that I didn't remember. She had a fine sense of humor for an overworked obstetrician, and smiled.

"Too bad. I thought she might be in labor — and we'd have a live demonstration for class. That's tonight's topic: Early Deliveries."

"Early Deliveries?" I said, full of new fears.

She took our arms, smiling. She didn't know what our

game was, with the throw-pillow approach to pregnancy, but she seemed to like us. "Just come on, you two. I'll talk slowly so you can memorize my every word."

Under a late February sky of lead and silver, Rose and I drove Bengal to Safariland. Sinclair, who was supposed to trailer him down, had come down with a hard case of the flu — but something more remarkable had happened to Sinclair lately. He and a bunch of old men from the Texas Pride parlor had gotten drunk one night and decided to kidnap Tammy Wynette. She was over in Ft. Bend County at the Cow Palace, and the old boys caught and blindfolded her late that night between the dressing room and her tour bus. All they did was drive her out to the prairie and make her sing "Stand By Your Man" a few hundred times, and for this crime they were never apprehended. It had plainly been the pinnacle of Sinclair's Second Adolescence, which meant life went downhill from there.

Two days later Claudine had taken him to the hospital, and though Dad said his pal only had "the whiskey-bottle flu," he was worried enough to skip the trip to Safariland. Shirley couldn't come with us either; she had an important date with Lawrence. They were going to discuss their "relationship." Since they were both psychology majors, they didn't have love affairs, just "relationships."

"She must be in love," Rose said, midway through our three-hour journey. Out of habit she'd been thinking about her daughter along the way. She missed having someone at home to argue with, especially now that she'd taken maternity leave.

"She says she is — but heck, Rose, he's so nice and handsome I'd love him myself, if I was that kind of guy. Hey, did I tell you why the cabanas are so cheap? They're a gay den. All the women there are trapped in men's bodies."

"Great," Rose moaned. "And naturally you got Shirley a room there?"

"Well, there's no safer place. And besides, I know all the guys. They're all right, and they're real excited about the baby. Homosexuals can't have any, you know."

"I know," Rose laughed. "My next boyfriend's going to be one."

"Oh?" I raised an eyebrow. "Already thinking of your next?"

Rose laughed. "No. No. No. Never again!"

I smiled and drove on. "That's what Shirley said, too. So just tell me where the line starts; I want to be at the front."

"Mr. Persistence," she said, and shook her hair. I couldn't tell whether she still loved me — we hadn't been together enough — but we certainly still liked each other. Her hair was cut back to shoulder length; she wore a loud purple muu-muu; her freckles looked lively today. Our friends from the cabanas had donated all their pillows, and Rose sat on a throne of them. She was having fun, an outing today. Lately the four walls of the house had begun to press in. Five weeks now, of maternity leave. But though she was enjoying herself, I was concerned.

"Are you-all doing okay? I'm not too sure you should have come. Dr. O'Keefe says —"

"Dr. O'Keefe doesn't know everything." She looked

with pleasure out the truck window; we were north of Eagle Lake now, on the expanses of Lisie Prairie. "You trust your Lamaze instructor too much."

"Why, don't you trust yours?"

"I did, up until Nancy's delivery. When we got to eight centimeters, she started to scream."

"Oh, God!"

Rose smiled. "We gave her epidural; she was fine."

I breathed again. Praise be to God for anesthetics. I planned to take plenty myself.

Rose changed the subject. "I saw that friend of yours — Penny Budlacek? — on *General Hospital* yesterday."

"You did? She's a movie star, with a name like that?"

"No," Rose smiled, "she calls herself Penny Buda now. She plays a former prostitute who's in love with an older man who's masquerading as his twin brother. It's all very complicated," Rose sighed, comparing *General Hospital* to the soap opera of her life. "And I'll be glad to get back to work."

Safariland was a sixty-thousand-acre preserve out of New Braunfels, fenced and cross-fenced to prevent large animals from eating the small. We stopped at the service gate and talked to the Saturday gamekeeper. He was a crabby old country fellow with an alcoholic's nose, about twice the age he should be to have this job. Mainly he was there to get bitten, so the rich owner wouldn't have to.

"Yeah, Mr. Crockett said you was acoming. He left a check here somewheres." He searched through several desk drawers before finding it. "Three thousand dollars — a lot of money for a boy."

"It's my college education," I said, putting the check carefully in my wallet.

"Yeah, if you want to spend it on that." He walked me outside to the truck, rum on his breath, and made a quick inspection to make sure Bengal was alive. He lay wind-whipped in the circus trailer, but when the old gamekeeper neared, he growled. The gamekeeper stepped back; he'd been bitten enough.

"Uh, yeah — you'll have to unload him yourself. I got to stay here for a load of chimpanzees. Just follow them signs to section 63B."

"How large a place will he have?" Rose spoke from the truck cab. She'd been uncomfortable for an hour and I'd forbidden her to walk.

The gamekeeper scratched his head under his hat. "A hundred, a hundred and fifty acres, I guess. Mr. Crockett wants to breed him to that crippled lion Josephine. Gonna get him a litter of them *ligers*, or *tions*, or whatever them half-breeds is called — just what a rich man needs, his own pet freak of nature. You just turn him loose out there."

Curious, I asked some more about this Josephine; was she the right gal for Bengal? She'd been crippled after she escaped and stepped in a jaw trap over in Hays County. She chewed off her foot to get free. "She weren't too hard to run down after that," the gamekeeper chuckled.

"How awful," Rose said, but she seemed to understand. When I climbed back in she was still thinking about it. I reached over and gave her hand a squeeze.

"Don't worry, honey. You won't have to chew off your feet."

She laughed. "That really puts my mind at ease."

We drove miles and miles through the park, through gates, cattleguards, and herds of gazelles, elephants, and springbok. Bengal had never seen such things before and crouched foolishly in his circus trailer, hoping for a tasty ambush. But like the other animals here, he would be fed regularly, and he would have nothing to do with his time but copulate. That's what most of the animals in the park were doing. At the last gate, which I got out to open so Rose wouldn't walk, a pair of grimacing ostriches were having congress. The veins on the bull's neck stood out; he flapped his useless wings and croaked, while the female clucked encouragement.

Rose stopped laughing abruptly, and shifted on her throne of pillows.

"Something wrong?" I got in.

"No, it's nothing. I just shouldn't laugh. Drive on."

The road came to an end at a large, lime-water pond, where a hippopotamus swam with her baby. The little fellow, shaped exactly like his mother only miniature, dove and porpoised while his mother ate her big lunch of plant life. I had planned a leisurely ceremonial picnic of sorts, setting my tiger free, but Rose's face had such an uncomfortable look that I hurried. The trailer door unlatched, I had to prod Bengal toward it. He was sniffing suspiciously at this large pool of water. At the door he hesitated again, his head out-of-bars, and sampled the outside air. The sky had cleared in Central Texas and the February sun seemed hard.

With an insecure growl Bengal dropped out of the door

on his forepaws, and with all the grace of a fluid he slinked over to investigate this pond. First his whiskers, then his paws — yes, this was very similar to the puddles in his cage. He eased himself in belly deep, then lifted his big, astonished head and roared.

Within another few minutes he was bounding around in the lily pads with such abandon that the hippo looked to her baby. The two of them crowded off in a corner while the crazy tiger swam in lazy circles. He already seemed at home in the water.

"Bubber," Rose said from the truck, her voice taut. "Bubber, we'd better go." When I got in she said, "We'll have to postpone the picnic."

On the long road out she consulted both a map and her wristwatch. I began to get very nervous, especially when she groaned, "Pull over."

"Oh, no!"

"Oh, yes."

"Not in the African Ruminants' section," I said.

"Find a shady spot," she replied.

I did, under a huge crooked mesquite tree, and lay my blanket out in the bahia grass. "No ants," I assured Rose as she stretched out consulting her watch. She seemed extremely confident herself, so I acted terrified. It seemed somebody had to.

"How long?"

"Shh." She counted seconds between contractions.

"The long car ride," I said. "And you always laugh too much. Soon?"

"Very," she said. "They're ninety seconds apart." She

lay back and thought. She was a nurse and could handle this; I was a young man and could not.

"What should I do? What should I do? I'll get help! I'll get help! You should have listened to your body."

"I did listen; it tricked me," Rose said, very calm, very definite. "Quit running around in circles. Go get the towels from the truck. And two pillows and the thermos of tea. It may be inconvenient, but it's going to happen."

Panting, I came to rest a moment and looked at Rose, her words sinking in. It *would* happen; a baby *would* be born. Right here. Right now. There was nothing we could do about it. We were trapped in another Force of Nature.

"Oh, God," I groaned.

"Move!"

"Don't worry!" I yelped, and ran to the truck for provisions. Nearby, the springbok had stopped springing and were grazing quite near us now. The mesquite shade smelled of their fertile droppings; this was their afternoon shade tree, not ours.

"What should I do?"

"You ought to lie down, too," Rose said.

I did, stretched out beside her. She hitched up her purple muu-muu.

"What *are* you mumbling?" she asked. "Prayers?"

"No—my last lesson at the Y. Don't worry, I've memorized everything."

"Good. Now tell me to relax, and breathe. I had Shirley in less than an hour."

"Oh, God," I said. "This is terrible. The waiting. I'm dying."

"Be quiet," Rose said. "We're in transition stage. Concentrate on your breath and your focal point."

Putting words in my mouth, she used me as a ventriloquist's dummy; I was glad to have some minor function. This seemed to last many hours.

"Pant. Pant. Pant. Blow!"

I panted myself silly, losing all track of time. Each contraction felt like a steep mountain, and each new peak seemed a little higher. Between mountains Rose rested and licked her lips. Sweat ran across her pale, freckled face. I'd never seen such a pretty sweaty, pale, freckled fat woman, but I moaned.

"Are you in pain?" she asked, amused.

"A little." I was trying to be brave.

Rose breathed in, pushed down, consulted her wristwatch. "You're right on schedule, then. Now remember, push down with each contraction."

I nodded, using my diaphragm and remembering my Lamaze on uterine contractions. Dr. O'Keefe hadn't said they'd be this painful. "Am I doing it right?"

"Sure. But your knees should be up. Like mine."

I followed Rose's example. Any moment I would have our baby.

After a while, we began to grunt as we pushed, then Rose said: "Bubber, I don't want to frighten you, but listen: I'm having the baby, right now. Wash your hands with the tea. And Bubber, hurry."

I jumped up and poured hot tea on my hands. "*Aught!*"

"Oomph! Ooomph!" Rose pushed down, then bit her lip. "Bubber, now I want you to settle down, and move between my legs." Her voice was tight; I moved. The cap of the baby's head showed! Rose grunted; I coaxed; slowly the baby appeared. She seemed like a little bubble rising. I put my hands on her hot wet living head.

I called back the progress to Rose. "The roots of her hair—Good Lord, she's got your hair! My forehead! Your eyes! Her nose! And oh damn—she's got my ears. They're immortal."

Rose smiled, still pushing. The herd of springbok had stepped closer to the mesquite shade, and they watched us, chewing their grasses. Strangely, I felt calm now; I gave Rose a ten-second rest, then asked her to push down again. This time I was able to bring our baby's shoulder out, and her short pink arm. Another heave, the other shoulder, and then my whole daughter slipped into view. Rose sat up immediately and held out her arms for the baby.

She wrapped it in a towel before I could count fingers and toes, and hugged the bundle softly to start the breathing. First mucus, then some bubbly hollering, followed by wet mewing as Rose put the baby to her bosom to nurse. Watching this I did a strange thing: I started to weep. I kept trying to talk, but I couldn't. A great, simple mystery had just been revealed to me, but every time I opened my mouth I wept louder. Finally I managed to say, "Thank you, thank you, thank you so much."

Rose smiled, pausing as she examined the baby. "You're welcome," she said. "But there's something else you should know about your daughter. She seems to have inherited your penis."

I stopped weeping and scooted up. It was true. Between my daughter's legs, she was a boy.

"Yes," I said, "I guess my penis is immortal, too."

Several springbok stepped closer to see.

Chapter

18

I HAD HOPED THAT THE BIRTHING ORDEAL WOULD weaken Rose enough that she would marry me, but afterwards I was the one who felt weak. We stopped on the way home at the hospital in Columbus, for me to take a sedative and for Rose and the baby to be examined. Two honest-looking obstetricians pronounced them exceptionally fit, and then our baby was weighed, measured, footprinted, blood-typed, and officially entered into the human race. Unfortunately we still didn't know which direction he would run.

Back home, the sedative wore off and I began to worry again. We were in Shirley's room, with Rose nursing the baby on the bed. I was pacing in front.

"Then what *is* going to happen to us?"

Rose had quit bothering to answer me. She was busy studying the baby, and eventually I stopped pacing to study him too. Though he was completely asleep, he sucked steadily with a deep, needy thirst. Basically that's all he did, eat and sleep, often simultaneously. Watching him, Rose's face took on the enormously contented look of a breastfeeding mother, which resembles a cow chewing cud. Vital fluids were flowing out of her body into his, making the moment seem important. She touched his big, little ear, and his wavy rose-colored hair.

"Dr. Kennedy said he'd never seen a baby with so much persistence," she said, amused. "I wonder where he gets that."

It touched me that *my* persistence was part of *his* chromosomes. There seemed a lot to discover about this baby; he was like a continent, waiting to be explored. Sitting on the bed I noticed that he instinctively held on to Rose's blouse, like a baby opossum clinging to its mother's hair. This instinct was part of man's ancient past, back when mothers had hairy chests and swung through trees. But this was a different, more complicated world, where hairless modern women couldn't be dominated by a man and his club. In this world, modern men had to whine to get what they wanted.

So I whined. "But, honey, you *have* to marry me now. . . . Please?"

"No," she said simply, "I don't." Then she added out of kindness, "Would you like to hold him awhile?"

I hadn't actually held him yet, and was afraid. "Aren't his bones still soft? What if his head falls off?"

Rose passed his little body to me anyway. "Just put your hand under it. Like that."

I stood up self-consciously rocking my sleeping son. He gurgled in a dream, and I gurgled back. What was he having, a womb-dream? In a few minutes I was rocking and gurgling like an expert, trying to penetrate his dream world. I wanted him to feel comfortable, cherished, and untroubled; I didn't want him to grow up as confused as me.

After a few more minutes I noticed something else about him. He didn't *just* eat and sleep.

"Honey, you better take him. I think he's had his first b.m."

Rose smiled, and while she changed him on the table in the corner, I came up behind her, my hands on her hips, my nose in her ear, the smell of a ripe baby around us. I sincerely loved this woman.

"Okay, okay," I said. "No more whining. Let's just talk short-range futures. What's your next move?"

The friendliness in my tone caught Rose's attention. She turned slightly to look at me, then turned slightly away. "Well, first I'm going to take a vacation, and think things over."

Since she was avoiding my eyes, I got suspicious. "A vacation? Where?"

"California. San Diego, with my brother Ben. He owns a stable of hunter-jumpers out there."

"But you'll come back?"

Rose returned to her evasive answers. "I don't know just yet. Now go get Shirley, will you? She's got to face me sooner or later."

Shirley had been afraid to see her mother; guilt was the reason, I suppose. After all, her bad-tempered schemes had caused all of this, and the evidence was now cribbed in her room. She'd recently taken up cigarette smoking and was exhaling tornadoes when I found her in the bathroom. From the door, I kidded her.

"Puncturing diaphrams again? Come on, I'm supposed to strong arm you if you resist."

Shirley took a last drag and dropped the butt in the toilet. "What kind of mood is she in? Does she hate me even worse than before?"

"No," I said, guiding her out by her small shoulders. "She never hated you. She's in a vacation mood, that's all."

I herded her into the room and watched from the door. She approached her mother and the baby timidly.

"Oh, Momma, he's so ugly," she said, in a soft admiring voice. Our baby, who had no teeth, looked like an old man.

"Would you like to hold him?"

"No." She thought about it. "Yes."

She cradled her little illegitimate half-brother with the bad instinct of a young father; that is, awkwardly and head down.

"Here," I said, "hold his head. Like that." I showed her how, then stepped back. "But don't hold him so close. You've been smoking cigarettes, and we don't want that imprinted on his tender brain too soon."

Shirley looked up; she hadn't heard me, gazing at the little guy. "What's his name?"

"We've finally decided," Rose said, "to call him Abe, after Bubber's mother."

"But his middle name is Shirley," I added, "after his partial father. Abe Shirley O'Leary-Drumm."

It seemed a very long name for such a little fellow, but it made Shirley smile. After all, a baby for whom she was partially responsible was being partially named after her.

"You two nuts," she said finally. "You really are a pair."

Later I walked Shirley outside for her return trip to Austin. I was going to help Rose with the baby for the first week, and then Shirley would have her turn. We walked arm in arm to the De Soto, the two fathers of a new human being. The February twilight spread out around us, and overhead, the pecan was beginning to bud. Shirley paused before getting into the car.

"But I'm not going to be as involved with fatherhood as you," she said. "Because Lawrence and I discussed our relationship, and Monday we're moving in together."

"You are? Congratulations!" After a hug, I held her at arm's length. "But you two get married soon. I don't want my co-father living in sin."

Shirley laughed, then looked me over thoughtfully. It was a tender look — the sort you give to somebody who's making a mistake. Then she stood on her tiptoes and kissed me, lightly on the ear. For almost a year she'd steered my fate; like a mother, she couldn't turn loose without giving some advice.

"Goofus, I guess even you can see what Momma's planning," she said.

"By going to California? Yes."

"Then you know that if she lets you come, it has to be *totally* her decision; if you force yourself on her again, she'll only grow to resent you. And both of you are too nice to deserve that."

"Oh heck, Shirley," I said, nudging her into the car. "How'd you get so mature?"

But I thought about her advice later, when Rose had

put the baby to bed and we went out to sit on the porch steps. Rose felt profoundly tired, with good reason, but she had some hard things to tell me. There was a stablehand's cottage on her brother's place, she said, where she planned to stay for at least a month. Maybe longer if she found out she still liked horses. And she hinted that she wasn't coming back.

"Well, that's all right with me," I said.

"It *is?*" She was surprised. "Aren't you going to put up a fight?"

"Nope. I'm through forcing myself on things. This morning I turned my tiger loose, and tonight I guess is your turn."

She rested her head wearily on my shoulder, and said, "Thanks."

I waited a moment before going on.

"But you ought to consider one thing. Out in California they don't have as many morals, so a couple like you and me might fit in."

She smiled sleepily and squeezed my hand. "It's nice to believe that," she said.

Then we grew quiet, listening to the geese honking out on the dark prairie, and worrying separately about the future. Actually, I did most of the worrying; Rose fell instantly asleep, and dreamed about our little boy. Every so often she would murmur in her sleep, commenting on the cute size of his feet.

And sitting there with my nose in her hair, I felt a powerful love for this Rose, and I didn't care a damn about our age difference or Dad's genetic explanation for that love. What was worse, I knew that in her deepest parts, Rose felt the same about me. The problem was in extracting that deep truth. Gradually I came upon an idea, though. I'd read in my Psychology class that when we sleep, our subconsciouses are slightly exposed. So I used this opportunity to question Rose's inner mind.

"I'm serious, honey. If you really want your freedom, I won't make you chew off your feet. Just tell me right now, do you want me to follow you out West?"

For a dramatic moment she stirred against my arm, then answered half in sleep.

"I don't want you to follow."

I sat awhile longer, thinking about what she'd said. But, really, it didn't take very long to come to one conclusion: Psychology was just a bunch of bunk.

One month later Rose and Abe left for California. Dad filled up her Pinto at the serpentarium, they all kissed goodbye, Abe hollered when they confined him in his car seat, and Dad slipped inside to call me long distance. I was still at college, though I'd convinced my professors to let me finish the semester by mail.

"She's leaving," Dad said. "She'll be passing your way in three hours."

"Okay, Dad. I'm ready. Thanks."

"Don't thank me. I just want my grandson raised in some kind of family, even an illegitimate one." Before he hung up, he added, "Good luck with the plan."

The plan was simple — to be standing on the shoulder of Highway 290 West when Rose passed. She would have the freedom to do with me what she wanted; but if she didn't pick me up, I hoped she'd at least have the good grace to run over me.

Out on the highway I caught an immediate ride on an empty hay truck. The driver, an old rancher turned alfalfa trucker, was the slow-thinking sort of fellow who mulls things over before saying a word. He watched me climb in — I was wearing only jeans and a T-shirt in the nippy March wind — and he listened as I described where I wanted to be dropped. This was any spot out of town that was bleak, windy, empty, and desolate-looking, preferably near the top of a hill. He thought about this for half an hour before coming to the wrong conclusion.

"Say fella, I know what you are," he said. "You're one of them escaped lunatics from the state mental hospital."

Lunatics often escaped from that facility, so this wasn't a completely strange assumption. Still, it startled me enough that I answered in the manner of a lunatic.

"No, no, no, no. Why did you think that? Do I look like one?"

The rancher examined me again. Fifteen minutes later he said, "Uh-huh."

But whatever he thought of me, he found me a great spot — thirty miles out, three-quarters of the way up a steep hill, surrounded by miles of the most eroded, overgrazed ranchland I'd ever seen. I climbed down and the old fellow handed me my cardboard suitcase. I thought I owed him an explanation.

"I'm gonna wait here for a very special woman to pass by."

Though I sounded very insane, the old rancher smiled.

"Well, don't worry, young fella. I won't tell a soul where you are. I'm a little crazy that way myself."

During the next three hours I discovered he wasn't the only one who made the wrong assumptions about me. Every passing motorist swerved out of my reach, thinking that if I wasn't a lunatic, I must be an escaped convict at least. Their low opinion of me gradually affected my opinion of myself. Here I was, an underclothed, big-eared boy shivering on a cold, bleak landscape, waiting for a woman who didn't want him. And sitting there on my suitcase, I suppose I had one of those existential flashes I'd read about, where Life seems a long tunnel with no light at the end.

I remember I was still sitting, hugging myself in the wind and wallowing in a sweet, dark self-pity, when I heard the approaching sound of a familiar engine. It was Rose, coming out of the valley below. Her hair was pulled back, and behind her our little red-haired, big-eared boy sat in his car seat, heavily asleep.

Rose didn't recognize me at first, and swerved away like all the other motorists; but she relaxed when she saw that the roadside lunatic was just me. I had jumped up so fast that I knocked over my suitcase, but I was trying to look like a man. My Dr. Graybow pipe hung from my lip for emphasis, and I held a small, simple sign. It read:

LAST CHANCE

Smiling, Rose looked at the sign and then at me, and slowed the Pinto automatically. Then she thought again and sped up. As she passed me I noticed a fine mix of sadness, good humor, and steadiness in her eyes, which I admired. Nevertheless, I wished she had stopped.

Turning, I watched her gain the crest of the hill, where I had propped up one of many, many more signs. This one read:

NEXT LAST CHANCE

Similar signs were placed at hundred-yard intervals down the other side of the hill for more than two miles. I didn't want Rose to miss her opportunity of a lifetime. And when she saw the two miles of signs flapping in the wind, she stopped the car to laugh.

The moment I saw her brake lights, the pipe fell out of my mouth. But when she stepped out of the car, smiled, and waved for me to come, I dropped everything else and broke into a run. It was a graceful, elegant run, I like to think, like a jungle animal joining his mate. I do have one regret about it, though. In my excitement I ran off without my suitcase, which both of us were too happy to notice. It was probably stolen shortly after we drove off, but in the story I tell my little boy, some other poor lunatic finds that suitcase and wears my clothes. I don't know why, but that ending always makes the little guy laugh.

Date Due

MAY 04 1991				
MAY 18 1991				
JUN 08 1991				
JUN 12 1996				

BRODART, INC.   Cat. No. 23 231   Printed in U.S.A.

Date Due

MAY 0 4 1991				
MAY 1 8 1991				
JUN 0 8 1991				
JUN 1 2 1996				